Dark Earth

By Jason Halstead

Prologue

"I'm getting nervous," Karen admitted, turning to her husband with a nervous smile.

Eric looked back at her, ignoring the snow covered Alaskan roads for a brief moment. He could not help but take a quick look at his beautiful wife, smiling as he looked into her eyes. He knew what she was going to say next.

"Are you sure you can take an entire season off?" she asked him.

He reached over and placed his callused hand reassuringly on her thigh. "Honey, we've got enough saved up. The season's only about four weeks, and they promised me there'd be a spot for me next season on the First Star. You know I can make up what one year off will do. Besides, there's other side work I can do to keep some money coming in."

"It's going to put it off though, you getting out of crabbing," she said with a frown. "It's so dangerous – I want you home with us all the time. I'm afraid just one season and I won't want you to go back."

Eric just smiled. He had gone to a few of the doctor's appointments and talked to plenty of veteran parents. He knew what she was going through and knew that she had been dealing with rampant hormones for eight months now. Let them get through one more and they would have a daughter. Then it would be just a few more weeks until her emotions were back on an even keel. It had been rough on him, but he knew it was worse on her. Besides that, she was worth it. "We'll do what we need to, don't you worry. It'll all work out."

The truth was that they had a lot saved up. Eric earned more in the four to six week crabbing season, catching Alaskan king crab and snow crab, than most guys earned in a year of steady work. Off season he would engage in salmon fishing or work on fixing boats if he couldn't find a job. After four years of this, they had a tidy bankroll saved away and plans for him to soon leave the dangerous life of crab fishing behind.

Eric enjoyed the work, and there were times when he still had a hard time accepting the thought of retiring. He was getting older though; he had been doing it since he was eighteen-and he was pushing twenty-two now. Still in his prime, he knew, but now he had to worry about his newlywed wife-and, in another month, their baby. He did not dare leave them alone in the world, he had to provide for them and be there for them.

He smiled at his young wife and said again: "It'll all work out for the best."

She nodded, sniffing back a tear, and smiled lovingly at him. Being with him made things seem all right. She believed him this time, just like every other time he told her the same thing.

Contrary to the words Eric had just spoken, however, disaster struck. Checking there was no cross traffic at the four way corner, he accelerated hard from the stop sign. Suddenly, from the opposite direction, a large truck came hurtling across the intersection, the driver pulling frantically at the wheel to try and avoid them. Unable to stop in the icy conditions, it slid sideways, turning partially, then caught just enough to flip it over. Eric slammed on his own brakes, useless in the snow, and cranked his wheel to the side to try and get away. His other hand shot protectively in front of his wife's chest even as she squeaked in terror at the impending collision. What happened next he would never remember, it was so chaotic and unimaginable.

When reality righted itself again, Eric blinked. He heard a horrible ringing in his ears and some distant noises that he could not identify. He could smell something too, -a mixture of gasoline, steaming anti-freeze, and melted rubber. He looked around, slowly recognizing the things he saw. He was in his truck, but the truck would never run again. The windshield was missing, save for a few chunks of crushed glass on the dashboard. He could see the remains of the other truck alarmingly close to him, steel melded with steel from the two vehicles. His side window was gone and a fresh but frigid breeze blew through it.

Eric's chest and left arm were numb one second, then in agony the next. He coughed a little, making him hurt even more. Something warm and wet was on his face and he felt a burning in his chest. He could just barely make out an arm streaked with blood sticking out of the other truck's front window; it, too, had been shattered. He wondered if the other driver was still attached to the arm or not.

He looked over and saw that his hand was still on Karen's chest, pinned to it by a piece of metal that had impaled both his hand and her chest. Her head hung limply over her chest, and both his hand and her shirt were red with blood.

"Karen," he said, half whispering and half croaking. "Hang in there baby, if you can hear me- please!"

He picked himself up a little, ignoring the agony in his ribs, and tried to bring his left arm around. It moved, barely, but he knew it was broken. He tried to ignore the pain as he reached over to her, but found his hand would not open or grip the metal that connected them.

"Don't move! Somebody called an ambulance," somebody yelled at him from his now open window.

Eric turned to look at them and heard them gasp. "Karen… my wife," he said. "Hurry! She's pregnant."

Eric felt his vision fading as he heard the man curse. He murmured as he passed out: "It'll all work out."

Chapter 1

I pulled my truck into my parking spot and looked around. The door burst open, and a grin made its way to my face as she came running out screaming, "Daddy!"

I climbed out of my heavy duty Chevy, happier than ever to be home, and swept my daughter up in my arms in a hug that spun her around before I set her back on the ground. "I'm back, Princess, how are you?"

She wrinkled her nose. "You stink like dead fish," she said.

I could only laugh. The innocence of children. Well, whatever innocence was left in a thirteen year old. I hoped she still had plenty of it to spare even though life had not been easy on her.

"It was good, we worked on some paintings in art class and..."

I listened attentively as she went on to gossip about school, enjoying everything she said and feeling complete again. Four days catching whitefish may not seem like much but it sure felt like it. I had been in the middle of the largest and most dangerous body of fresh water in the world, while all that was left of my life was waiting on dry land.

Thirteen years previously, my wife, Karen, had been declared dead when we reached the hospital after a car crash. CPR performed by the paramedics had kept her blood pumping with enough oxygen to allow an emergency c-section to deliver our daughter. She was premature and had a rough time of it, but from the very beginning she proved herself to be too full of life to accept defeat.

I was only there because of an understanding paramedic who pushed me in on a cart. I had refused to be treated until I found out what happened with my wife. It left my heart feeling as though a vice was squeezing the life out of it, as I found out what happened to her. I wanted to give up and just die myself.

Young and stupid, I could not imagine life without her. I had met Karen when I first flew out to Dutch Harbor. She was a waitress in the seediest bar there, the Latitude. We hit it off instantly; it was just meant to be. Four years later we were married and pregnant and though we had our share of worries we always knew we would have each other to rely on through life. We had the kind of relationship that sickens others. Too good to be true. I guess it was.

A nurse showed me my daughter after she had been cleaned up. I was a mess and in no shape to hold her, but something happened to me when I saw her. Still horribly sad, something lifted in me and changed. I knew I had to hang on and fight. My wife was gone, but here was someone else that depended on me. Someone defenseless and innocent. Tears were streaming from my face because of so many emotions hitting me, but for once I did not care whether it made me less manly or not.

"Jessica," I had whispered. It was the name my wife wanted for her. We had playfully argued all along about names, though I always knew I would give in. I just liked giving her a hard time. If there was nothing else I could do for Karen, I could at least make certain that her daughter had the name that she had chosen for her.

"Daddy!"

I snapped out of my reverie, sniffing a little at the memories, and smiled. I got a little choked up every time I came home from a fishing trip. It was nothing like the old days, crabbing in the Bering Sea and hoping to escape injury or worse. Jessica and I packed that up before she was two and left for safer waters. Literally. I came back home to Northern Michigan and bought myself a fishing boat with the money Karen and I had saved up.

"Just daydreaming about how pretty you are, sweety," I said to her. It was true too, she was a beautiful little girl. A beautiful young lady, I corrected myself. She was a teenager now.

She smiled in spite of her anger, happy to be flattered. "Sooo, Justin asked me if I would be going to the lumberjack dance."

I raised an eyebrow. Apparently I wasn't the only one that thought she was pretty. "A little young to be dating, don't you think?"

She rolled her eyes and sighed. I had to fight to keep from laughing at the expression. "Daddy, it's not a date! Besides, he's fourteen already."

The lumberjack dance was a school event so I was hardly concerned. Plenty of chaperones. Besides, my little darling was sure to be the belle of the ball. Proud? Sure I was, but with due cause. She was top of her class in everything, from math to English to band and choir and art. With a grin I liked to tell everyone she got those genes from me. So what if she showed no interest in sports? As far as I was concerned she was perfect.

"So? Can I go?"

I sighed theatrically. "This is next Friday?"

She nodded excitedly. "Well, are you going to have your chores done? How about your homework?"

"It's a week away!" she protested.

"Just being proactive," I teased. "I'll be sure that I'm back to take you, I promise."

She threw her arms around me and hugged me tightly. I relished the affection. Rugged fisherman or not, there's just something about a hug from a little girl that can not be denied.

I opened the door and was met by the happy woof of our dog, Mozart. Mozart was a golden retriever that Jess had picked out when she was six years old. Like every dog out there, he was as much a member of our family as any of us were.

Petting him and talking to him in my doggy-voice, the one where you get excited and talk like a two year old, we moved in and Jessica sat down at the kitchen bar. "So what's for dinner?" I asked, heading behind it to look for food.

"Mozart and I already ate," she said. "Turkey sandwiches."

"Mozart?" I asked, frowning.

She smiled and shrugged, adopting an innocent look that I could not be mad at. "Dog eats better than I do," I muttered, turning to open up the fridge and seeing a spare turkey sandwich in a plastic baggy for me. I chuckled and took it out, then turned and waggled a finger at her. She giggled.

Stupid and corny, but those were the moments that I cherished most in my life.

"How's the propane holding up?" I asked her, glancing out a window towards the big propane tank we had. It was our source of just about everything there. I had a generator for emergency electricity, but mostly we used propane for everything since the power company had not run electricity up our road as far as we were yet. They kept telling me next year they would do it, but year after year went by, and they still hadn't.

We lived North of Marquette, NorthWest, actually, on county road 510. Most of the traffic we saw was logging trucks. That and occasional tourists-not many people were crazy enough to live up here. Rugged terrain and seasonal roads often blocked by snow meant we seldom had any visitors, especially the kind we had not invited ourselves.

"Down to a third of the tank," she said. "You should probably order some more."

I grunted, my mouth full of sandwich, and figured I would do so tomorrow. It was getting dark, especially up North in late September. I took a drink of water and looked at the fireplace. "No fire?" I asked her.

"Oh my gosh! I forgot to start it!" She seemed to think it was a major oversight.

I just chuckled.

"Indian summer, I'll get it. You get distracted or something? Thinking about Justin and the dance, maybe?"

"Daddy!" she admonished me. "No, it wasn't cold so I was working on some drawings. The painting we did this week in class gave me some new ideas to try out."

"Oh? Can I see them?" I asked her, genuinely curious.

Jessica could do things that took my breath away and made me wonder how she managed to be so talented. I was just an average man with an average job. Her mother, wonderful in her own way and more special to me than any other woman alive, had been no more gifted than I was. Jess, on the other hand, had never found something she could not do and do well.

"Sure, stay right there!" She was off like a shot, heading across the open floor of our log cabin and into one of the two rooms at the end, her private sanctuary. The other room was my office. Upstairs, in a partially open loft, was my bedroom.

Outside, we had an outhouse. It was a composting one, thankfully, so it seldom required any work to be done on it. It was almost completely odor free as well. Of course my idea of odor free and Jessica's differed, as she would remind me with her nose crinkled every time she used it or made mention of it.

She came back now with some large papers. I'd invested in some quality sketching paper, at her request, and now I could see why she'd wanted it. I forced myself to swallow my final bite of sandwich before I let my mouth hang open in wonder.

"You like?" she asked me guardedly.

I nodded mutely, then stared a minute longer at them. They were so realistic I would have sworn they moved. The first one was my boat on a calm sea with the sun setting behind it. The level of detail took my breath away. Especially since she had used colored pencils and made it even more realistic with color.

"This is… incredible," I told her, at a loss for words.

"I haven't finished this one yet," she said, showing me a landscape picture.

I identified it almost immediately, it was that good. "The view from Hogsback?" I asked her.

She nodded. Hogsback was the name of a nearby peak that was a couple of hours hike from the nearest road and about ten miles from our place. Although it was only a mile or so up, it was still a mildly challenging hike and climb. We tried to make a day of it at least once a month, sometimes more. It was the tallest mountain in the area. All that mattered was that you could see for miles from it and it was a beautiful place to be.

"You're amazing," I said, looking back at the picture. I was unable to explain my feelings any other way.

She smiled happily and gave me a hug, then took the Hogsback picture back towards her room.

"Don't you want this one?" I called out to her.

"That's for you," she said over her shoulder.

I just stared at it and decided I needed to have it framed. More than fatherly pride, it stirred up things in me that I could not explain. There was something to it, an energy or something. Drawing was like music and dancing had been for her; just another thing she could master with time and practice.

Shaking my head at her many talents, I called out to tell her I was going to grab some firewood. Outside I walked over to the stacks of chopped wood and picked up some smaller pieces off the top to make kindling out of them. With no electricity and not wanting to spend too much on propane, firewood was the way to go. When I was home I would typically even cook dinner on the woodstove-or grill it outside in our campfire ring.

I supported the illusion of being a gruff mountain man by having spent more than a decade living on the edge of civilization. I liked to think I had picked up a fair amount of affinity for nature. Between fishing and living a rough life, I was in great shape, but more than that, I was in tune with my surroundings well enough to know that something seemed amiss. I blamed myself for being distracted by Jessica's artwork for not noticing it sooner.

Axe in hand, I turned around slowly, trying to look casual but probably failing since I had a suspicious glare in my eyes. I found it pretty quickly-there was a black and expensive looking SUV parked in the road. There were a lot of trees between it and me, as they had not parked near the driveway. I don't know why, but for some reason it just seemed very wrong. Axe still in my grasp, I headed for the house. I felt a sudden urge to make sure that Jess was safe. The urge turned to near panic. My stomach clenched and my heart started to race.

A bark from Mozart followed by a scream spurred me into action. My body flew on autopilot while my brain refused to consider what could be wrong. I flung myself through the door and saw Jess emerge from her bedroom. She was not alone. A man was behind her, holding her with his arm around her neck and a gun at her head. I came to a stop, hesitating again as my brain tried to catch up with my body. My eyes went to Jess. She had a wide-eyed look that I knew meant she was terrified and frantic. He had a solid grip on her. I looked around, wondering if there were any others and wondering who he was and why he had her. None of it made sense, I was a fisherman and she was just a girl in junior high school. Why would anybody want to hurt her?

My eyes went back to the guy holding her. I had nothing special, especially not at the house. My money was in the bank, there was nothing here, not even a television. I knew it could not be a simple robbery. I stared at him, trying to understand and I knew there was something about the man that was nagging at the back of my mind.

"What do you want?" I asked carefully, not letting him know how out of control I was. I realized I had forgotten to leave the axe outside, and I wondered if he might consider it a threat and hurt her because of it.

"I'm truly sorry," was all he said.

He looked down at Jess and somehow I knew what was about to happen. Terror gripped me, there was no way I could lose her too.

"NO!" I shouted, starting towards him.

I knew I would never make it in time. Jess, somehow, knew as well. She tried to twist and pull away even as I risked everything and threw the axe. The gun fired. There was a silent rushing of air and a click as the chamber ejected the spent shell casing. No wonder the barrel had been so long; it was silenced. In spite of my strangled cry and the sound of my feet thudding into the floor I distinctly heard the brass casing hit my wood floor and roll across it.

Jessica fell, lying on the ground with her beautiful brown hair covering her face. I could see blood already. I focused on the redness of it until everything I saw was tinted.

The man was off balance from where the handle of the axe had hit him across the chest. I slammed into him full on and sent him crashing back into the wood stove. Cast iron, it weighed hundreds of pounds. With him breaking my fall, we managed to push it back and knock it over, spewing ashes and knocking it free of the chimney. The gun was on the floor, knocked free from the impact of my axe. I only wished the bladed end had struck first.

He rolled away, cradling his arm from which blood dripped. His own, not my daughter's. He ran from me, not stopping to grab his gun as he saw me lunging back to my feet to chase him. He fled through the open door and it was there that I hesitated, breathing hard and feeling light headed and numb. Jessica had fallen, I saw her blood. She had been shot in the head. What hope did I have but revenge?

I went to her anyway, my hands already digging for the cell phone in my pocket. Technological backwater that it was, I still had a few bars of service on my cell phone. I crouched next to her, mouth dry with fear of what I might find. I suspected the worst. In fact, I knew it would be over. The beautiful life that was all I had left was gone to spend eternity with her mother. I could only hope that Karen would take better care of her than I had.

Tears running down my face, I reached down to pull Jessica's hair back so I could, at least, gaze on her face before it grew stiff with rigor mortis. I felt her blood on her hair and I could smell it, coppery and hateful. If I never saw blood again, it would be too soon.

She looked so peaceful. Beautiful, really. I felt dead inside-numb, and as though I was on the edge of a bottomless pit. The bullet must not have passed through because there was no exit wound on the side of her head facing me. For a brief second my hopes lifted, soared really. I thought for a foolish second that maybe he had missed, then I remembered the gun pointing at the other side of her head. And if he had missed, why was there blood; why was my daughter lying still on the floor? My hopes crashed and I felt myself teetering on the edge of the cliff of despair again.

I sagged back, limp and nearly falling to the floor in defeat. The sadness washed away as a fresh surge of rage filled me, making my muscles tense and my eyes dilate. I rose to my feet and tore off through the open door. At the end of my driveway I saw the suburban tearing down the dirt road back towards Marquette. I memorized the license plate and flipped open my phone. I dialed 911 even as I ran to my truck, intending to follow him. I wanted to run him off the road. I wanted to catch him and beat him and demand that he tell me why. I wanted to kill him. I had never in my life wanted vengeance against somebody so bad. I had never wanted death so clearly that it pervaded my body and I could taste the ugly sweetness of it.

I dropped the keys, cursed thickly, and tried again to shove them in the ignition of the truck. Something calmed me then, just enough for me to ignore the single purpose my existence had taken. I hesitated and I listened and heard it again. It was Jessica, calling for me.

Thinking it a delusion, I stumbled from the truck and fell, dropping my phone. I climbed to my feet and rushed back inside, certain I was going crazy. There she was, sitting up with one hand to her head, and sobbing. Feeling like I was not even in control of my body, I all but crashed into her. I held her and hugged her and kissed her and did not care about the blood or the stranger or anything. As messed up as the day had been, it was suddenly the best day of my life. She was alive!

"Daddy, it hurts," she sobbed against me.

I pulled back just enough to look at her. "Shh," I whispered, my voice so tight with emotion anything else was impossible. "Let me see it, honey."

She cried harder when I pulled her hair back and looked at the side of her head. She had twisted just enough that the bullet had only grazed her skull. I could see the bone, but it did not look broken. There was a lot of blood too, though I knew it was not arterial. I remembered my phone, the call sent but me not there to tell the man on the other end what was going on, and fought the urge to let go of her and run and get it. Holding her, right then, was the only reason I had to be alive at that moment. The phone could wait.

"It'll be okay, Jess, I promise. This will all work out," I told her, holding her close to me again.

We just stayed there, her finding shelter from the terror and the pain in my arms and me clinging to what little sanity I had remaining by holding her. Soon enough the police and an ambulance showed up, and they found us clinging to one another on the floor.

Chapter 2

Jessica spent the night in the hospital. They stitched together her scalp and gave her plenty of pain medication for the concussion. I just paced back and forth when I was not with her. I chewed my nails, I clenched my fists, and I felt like pulling out my hair in reaction to the many emotions rushing through me. I realized later that night that my hand ached. I blamed it on the recurring soreness I had in my left wrist. Ever since the car accident where Karen had died I had a few lasting reminders. A sore wrist from where it had broken, occasional ache in my ribs from where they had been broken, and the scar on my right hand through the middle of my palm to the back of my hand.

This time, though, my fingers were swollen, so it had nothing to do with a past injury. Since we were at the hospital, I asked a nurse to check it out. Nearly an hour later I had a splint on the first two fingers on my left hand; I had broken them tackling the would-be assassin. Adrenaline is an amazing thing, numbing an injury that a few hours later felt like it would be impossible to ignore.

I could not figure out what the deal was with the man who had attacked us, nor why every time I thought about him something bothered me, like I should have known him. The cops had questioned me at length, taking the pistol on the floor as well as some of the blood that he had dripped over the floor and on the stove. They even dug the nearly fatal bullet out of the floor. Somehow through it all, even though we had been attacked, they made me feel like I was guilty for it. The tone of their questions and the questions themselves haunted me, making me second guess myself even though I knew I was right. I was still wondering if I had told them everything, they left still acting like I was hiding something from them.

Mozart was dead. We had large windows in the house and they were often open to let fresh air in. It had been warm all week so our windows had been open. The intruder had cut through the screen and shot the dog, which had been what caused Jess to scream. Holding her at gunpoint, he emerged out into the main room. I'm certain now his intent had been to keep her hostage to make sure he knew where I was, then shoot us both.

I kept running the words he had spoken to me through my head, "I'm truly sorry," wondering what the point of that was? He tried to kill my daughter–no amount of "sorry" would ever make up for that. The fact that he did kill our dog was a painful reminder that his attack had been serious. Our privacy and security had been violated, our best friend taken from us; how would we ever feel safe again?

I had to call Jake the next day. Jake Tenyke was my first mate and best friend. I let him know we wouldn't be going out that week, and ended up telling him the entire story. Jessica and I ended up heading over there after we took care of a few things at home. After spending some time there I tried to leave Jess behind, but she knew I was trying to get away. She must have sensed it in my attitude, because I found her following me even as I thought I had made a clean getaway.

"Where are you going?" she asked. She wore a ball cap to hide the bandage on her head, but the lost look on her face and the weakness in her voice pulled at me.

"I just need to run a few errands," I lied. Technically it was an errand I had to run, but it still felt like a lie. She nodded, but stood there staring at the ground. "Jess…" I did not know what to say to her.

"Can I come?"

I sighed. "Its paperwork, honey, you'd be bored."

"I could use a little bored. Besides," she added, "I want to say goodbye to him."

Mouth open, I just stared at her. How did she know? I clenched my fists in silent frustration. Not frustration with her, but with the jerk that had tried to ruin our lives. In a way, he had succeeded, even if we still lived.

"All right, come on," I told her, turning and opening up my truck door.

She hurried around to the other side, her arms hugging herself as though she was cold. It was cool out, but she had a warm sweater on.

"Thank you," she said after she had climbed up and buckled her seat belt.

I nodded, unable to think of anything to say

We ended up at our veterinarian. After a brief but very painful wait in the lobby we were escorted back in to see the doctor. He greeted us solemnly, offering condolences on our loss. Sure, it was only a dog and I kept telling myself that, but it still left my knees a little weak and my stomach empty. Tears, which she had valiantly managed to hold back, rushed down Jess's cheeks when he presented an urn to us with Mozart's ashes in it. Jessica took it silently and waited for me to sign some papers. Back in the truck she broke down into sobs and I found my own cheeks wet as well. It was several minutes before she scooted back to her side and I was ready to start up the truck so we could leave.

As much as losing the dog hurt, it was seeing what it did to Jessica that really made me feel like a failure. Mozart had been her friend and confidant, the one who was there when I was not. I asked her if she would like another dog and she just shook her head, unable to speak. It was too soon.

Logically I knew that the attack was not my fault; Mozart's death was out of my control. That logic did not help assuage the grief I felt for what we both were going through, however. I kept finding myself thinking about what-if scenarios. What if I had noticed the SUV sooner? What if…? I always stopped myself because I knew there was nothing I could have done differently. I learned not to play that game after Karen died. It was a lesson I had hoped never to need again. It's funny, in a not so funny way, how reason and emotion can disagree with each other.

Our peace shattered, Jessica and I found comfort in Jake's family. Surrounded by warmth, we sucked it in and tried to remind ourselves that not all of the world was a harsh and cruel place. She seemed to heal quickly, both inside and out. As in everything she did, I was proud, impressed, and a little bit amazed. Her smiles came more often and she even started to joke with me again. I was envious of it and tried to play along. I had always had a hard time letting go and moving on-the stubborn way I held onto my wife's memory was a fine example of that.

Desperate to try and make things normal again for us, I took her to the school dance that Friday. I would like to say I was a trusting and unconcerned parent, but the truth was that I was a nervous wreck! I ended up sitting in my truck outside the school the entire time, looking anxiously at any shadow or movement I saw. Everything looked like a man with a gun to me, and for the life of me I still could not understand why we had been attacked.

When the dance was over she came outside and the hairs stood up on the back of my neck. Now would be the time, I reasoned. A man with a rifle could drop her easily as she walked amongst her friends, and there would be so much confusion no one would be able to know what had happened. I craned my neck viciously, trying to spot the imaginary assailant as panic began to rush through me. I had to move, had to get out and I had to get her and protect her.

The truck door opened and she climbed up and in. I turned to look at her and very nearly hugged her. She gave me a 'what gives' look and immediately started chatting about her night at the dance. Pure girl talk. I listened politely and kept her going where necessary. My mind was really on the mirrors and windows, wondering when and where the next attack would come from. My heart had slowed from the frantic pace my panic had sent it into to something that was still dangerously close to a heart attack level.

The following Monday Jessica went to stay with Jake's family. I had to take the boat out, not only did I have contracts to fill, but both Jake and my two deckhands needed a paycheck. Come to think of it, a steady paycheck came in mighty handy for me too.

My phone rang as we were loading bait onto the boat early that morning. I tossed on the coil of rope I had in my good hand and scrounged through my pocket to get the phone. I answered it just in time before it went to voicemail and listened to the detective who had been assigned my case.

He wanted me to come in so he could talk to me, but I told him I was headed out for a few days fishing. He insisted, and so did I. He finally convinced me when he asked me if I had recognized my attacker. Something clicked, even though I could not place just what it was. I just knew that that nagging feeling was justified. Annoyed at myself for not being able to draw a line between the dots, I agreed to meet him and hung up.

"Jake, I hate to do this, but you've gotta take the boat out," I told my first mate.

He looked at me, curious, then grinned. "Sure thing skipper," he said. "Don't worry, we can handle it."

"I know you can," I said, clapping him on the back. "That's what I'm afraid of-soon you guys are going to figure out you don't need me!"

Jake laughed and the other two looked up at us, wondering what was going on. Jake winked at me, letting me know he understood. My deckhands were good guys, but I had only brought them on a few months ago when the last two I had went back to college. Not the kind of people I felt comfortable sharing my personal problems with.

At the station I instantly felt nervous and guilty again. I tried to shake the feeling but figured that everything from the way the place was built to the way the police interacted with me was designed to keep me on the defensive. When I reached the detective's office he had me sit down and smiled almost apologetically at me. We talked, briefly, but it did little to smooth my ruffled feathers. He pushed a folder across his desk to me and asked me to open it up.

I found myself looking at mug shots of the guy whose prints matched the ones on the gun. My blood felt like ice in my veins as I stared at the name and the face of our attacker: Johann Pederson. He looked different, but he was the same guy. The pictures were thirteen years old. I saw the date on them and looked up, my mouth open. I saw the man and then I saw him, in my mind. I remembered looking around from the front of my truck in Alaska and seeing the wrecked truck that had hit us. It had rolled a complete circle by the time it hit us, and I saw the man's face, unconscious though he was, against a cracked window.

"Mr. Baxter? Eric?"

I heard the words and knew that the detective was speaking them. Reacting to them, that was an entirely different thing. I felt like I was floating in the eye of a giant storm. Smooth waters beneath me, but waves threatening on every side big enough to plunge me to the bottom and leave me there.

"He killed my wife," I finally whispered, finding some way out of the maelstrom in my mind.

The detective nodded. "It was ruled vehicular manslaughter, but an accident. The brake lines on his truck had frozen and snapped."

"I remember," I said numbly, then I looked up at the detective. "I never even knew his sentence, I assumed it was an accident. I had to go on living, you know? I had a daughter to take care of…"

"He was out in seven years for good behavior," Detective Shade told me. "No priors, and nothing afterwards either. No sign of him anywhere, near as we can tell. Now he's shown up here."

"Yeah, he showed up," I repeated, finding myself staring at his picture again and wanting to understand why.

"What does he want?" I asked, at a loss.

The detective shook his head. "I'm sorry, I don't know. You've never seen him or talked to him?"

"Just the one time."

"I've already sent his picture out, we're looking for him, but until we pick him up, do you have any friends you can stay with?"

I nodded and sighed. I was a mess and I knew it. "I came up here to be alone. To be left alone and to live a quiet peaceful life. I wanted my daughter to have a fresh clean life, never to be reminded of what happened."

"I want that too, Mr. Baxter," he said. "We'll pick him up…he'll make a mistake sooner or later. This may be the back woods, but we've got good people up here, people that care. We'll find him."

I nodded and stood up, not sure of where I was going or how I was going to get there. "Thirteen years," I whispered. "What could make a man hate that much?"

He stood up with me and shrugged. The question was rhetorical but I guess he felt he owed me an explanation. Maybe he felt bad for how the police had treated us, even though they had not done anything wrong. "If you figure that out then let me know, we'll figure out how to stop a lot of crime."

I left the precinct and went straight home. On edge, I walked around the house and my one hundred twenty acre property wondering if anything was different. It seemed unmarred, but I was still wary when I entered the house. Everything was as it should have been. I thought I imagined a few things misplaced, but I realized I was probably just being paranoid. Amazing what being stalked by a cold blooded murderer will do to your sanity.

Jess had some things in a bag already over at the Tenykes'. I grabbed some more clothes for her, random stuff really, and pretended not to pay any attention when I went through her underwear drawer. I felt dirty, touching her things, even though she and I had been doing laundry together for years. Somehow this seemed weird, since she always took care of her own unmentionables. My heart nearly stopped when I saw a couple of thongs she must have purchased on her own. Thirteen and wearing thongs? Where had my little girl gone?

I left those in the drawer and moved on, grabbing shirts, pants, socks, sweaters, whatever she might need. I figured we needed to be somewhere else while this manhunt went on, somewhere where the man being hunted was not. The only place I could think of was Jessica's grandparents, Karen's parents, in Seattle.

I spent the remaining few hours of the day waiting outside of her school. She was surprised to see me, since I should have been fishing, and looked around nervously as though she knew something was wrong. She climbed into the truck and gave me, 'the look'. The look that demands an explanation and won't settle for anything less than the whole truth.

I told her everything I knew; I figured it was her neck on the line as much as mine, she deserved to know. Her question was the same as mine, "Why?"

"I don't know, honey. I don't understand it any more than you do. I've never made any enemies and neither had your mom. None of this makes any sense."

"Maybe it was somebody that liked mom and was upset that you got her?" she asked, staring thoughtfully into space.

"You've been reading too many teen romance books," I said, shaking my head and chuckling at the suggestion in spite of how frayed my nerves were.

"You buy them for me," she countered.

Having no planned trip or itinerary, the trip to Seattle took five days of serious driving. Jessica bore up well, hiding her boredom by drawing or playing games. Sometimes she hummed or sang, others she chatted with me. It certainly helped, because I was staring in the mirror behind me most of the way, expecting to see Johann pulling up behind me with a gun. Other times I daydreamed about a car coming over the line and slamming into us-not so unlike what happened the first time my life had been nearly jerked from me like a fish biting a juicy worm on a hook.

Instead we made it to Seattle with no harm done. The bags under my eyes and nervous glances around and behind me showed how my nerves were frayed to breaking, but that was as much my own fault as anybody's. Jessica and I stood at the door, bags in hand, and waited until it was opened by a very surprised Frank Sparks, my father-in-law.

"What the…well hi there!" he said, surprised, but evidently happy to see us. Frank had been a plumber and was now retired. His only complaint in life, at least as far as he told me, was that he did not get to see his grandchildren enough. Jessica was one of three, the other two belonging to my late wife's younger brother, Jimmy. They lived in Houston.

"Susan, you're not going to believe this," he called out even as he was spreading his arms to give and receive hugs from Jess.

Susan, my mother-in-law, showed up a few moments later. Her confused expression turned to surprise and then excitement. She pushed grandpa out of the way so she could get her own hug from Jessica, then finally offered me a hug too.

"Eric, you're early–we weren't expecting you two for a few more months," Frank said. "What's going on?"

Normally we visited during the holidays. Lake Superior ices over and my boat can't handle the flows, so we take the winters off. What better time to visit family? Especially since my own has been shrinking. My parents split up when I was young; in fact my dad left before I was born. My mom died three years back, cancer from smoking and drinking too much. Frank and Susan had always treated me like their own, and Karen's death hadn't changed that. Even for a tough fisherman like me they made it hard to hide behind a gruff exterior.

"Yeah, well, we needed an early break," I told him, smiling but with enough edge to it so he'd let it drop.

Susan missed the look. "Your school's not over yet, is it honey?"

Jess looked up at me and I just shrugged. "Not yet, grandma," she agreed.

There was an awkward moment of silence, then Susan recovered and said, "Well this is silly, come in! I'll make up some beds for you guys, looks like you brought enough to stay for a little bit."

I smiled graciously and helped Jess head in, carrying both her heavier bags and mine. Grandma followed up immediately with a late dinner. Something about grandmas, they always insist on feeding you. Not that we were complaining-we were both pretty hungry because we had not wanted to waste time by stopping for food on our last day.

It was not long after when Jess was nodding off on the couch. We made small talk the entire time, catching up on how the fishing had been, how school had been for her, what the weather was like, everything families parted by distance talk about when the distance is covered. Now, though, I knew things were going to get awkward.

I roused my daughter up and led her to her bedroom. She laid on the bed and I told her not to worry about pajamas, just crash as she was. She smiled and gave me a sleepy hug and a kiss, then added, "Are you going to tell them?"

I nodded and smiled. "They deserve to know, honey."

"Good, I hate secrets," she said, then curled up on her side and was asleep in moments.

I backed away, amazed again at the spark of brilliance that was my daughter. I was sure every father felt that way about their own kid, but for some reason I had a hunch mine really was extra special.

Back in the living room I sat down and smiled at them both, then leaned forward, elbows on my knees and hands together. "So, want to know the real reason we're here?"

That got their attention. Both burst out with nods and requests for information. I chuckled nervously and began.

"Did Karen have any enemies?" I asked, jumping straight into it. "I'm asking because what happened before, when Karen died…it happened again."

Susan's eyes widened and her hand went to her mouth. Frank frowned.

"You were in another car accident? Your truck looked okay? Are you guys all right?"

"No accident, Frank. Not now and not then, either."

"Wait a minute," he said, confused. "Start at the beginning."

I nodded, and explained everything to him. It choked me up a few times at the memory, and at other times I felt myself growing angry and my tone rising. I tried to control it and lower it down, but I saw my emotions mirrored on the faces of my in-laws. When I finished, although it was only a few minutes later, I felt a sudden weariness, as though I had just personally pulled in a record size sturgeon with a fishing pole and now my body felt it was time to collapse and recover.

Frank and Susan almost exploded, wondering who he was, why he was after us, and just what was going on. I listened as patiently as I could, giving them pretty much the same answer for every question: "I don't know."

"So, did Karen have any enemies? Any rivalries? Anything at all you can think of?" I asked again, even thinking briefly of Jessica's farcical theory of a jilted would-be lover.

They shook their heads. Nothing came to them. Karen had always been kind and friendly, never wanting anyone mad at her. That was the same Karen I remembered. Faultless, socially speaking. I sighed and rubbed my tired eyes.

"It's exhausting, being stalked," I told them with a weak smile. "Looks like I'll need to invest in a couple of bulletproof vests for a while," I added.

"How did they find you? I mean, you're not hiding up there, but no electricity or phone, just a P.O. Box for an address," Frank wondered aloud.

I shrugged. "Maybe they followed me from the docks," I said. It had occurred to me before, but prior to the attack I had no reason to be suspicious of any cars behind me. Maybe I would have seen him had I looked behind me on that day.

Susan's face went paler than it had been already and her hand covered her mouth again. Frank and I both looked at her, me with a sudden suspicion.

Frank asked, "What did you do?"

"Someone called a while back, a few months. He said he was a distant relative; he even told me some proper names and information to confirm it. He claimed he was looking for family tree info, trying to contact people to send out some things. I gave him your address, Eric–well, the P.O. Box, I wouldn't give him your phone number."

Frank muttered something under his breath. I smiled at Susan reassuringly and waved it off. "It's a good thing you did that, actually. Imagine if he'd found my home address? He might have got there before I was home."

She put her face in her hands and started to cry. I hurried over to her and put my hand on her back consolingly. "Susan, it's okay. We are okay. If it had not happened this way, it would have happened some other time, another way. And maybe I would not have been able to stop him."

I looked at Frank for some help. "Eric's right, Susan. " Some help he was.

"It'll all work out for the best. The police know who to look for, after all, because of it. Besides, after the last week I can say that if I spent the rest of my life living on the lam, hiding from some crazy killer, I would go crazy myself. This way it will be rough, but we'll be through it much quicker."

She sat up a little, sniffing and reached for a tissue to blow her nose. "I'm so sorry, Eric, I was sure he was related. Everything sounded right."

I shrugged. "Who knows, maybe he was? Maybe Johann found out about us some other way." Frank rolled his eyes, but fortunately his wife was not looking his way. "Jess knows everything, okay, so don't be afraid to talk to her about it. She's an amazing kid, really. I couldn't ask for anything better than her. I'm so proud of everything she does it makes me think I'm overbearing and crazy sometimes!"

Susan smiled and laughed a little. Frank chuckled understandingly. "She's pretty special," he admitted. "I'll call you a liar if you ever say anything, but I've been pretty impressed a few times myself with her–more than the other grandkids."

"My lips are sealed," I said with a smile. "Tell you what, since I'm bragging, you have got to check this out!"

I took off without warning, heading back to the bedroom I had stored my things in. It had been Karen's room, years and years ago. I stayed in there every time I visited, and I'll admit I spent my share of time the first couple of occasions going through her closet and boxes hoping for something, anything really, that would have her scent on it or spark some memory. Now it was pretty much my room when I visited; other than pictures and a few decorations for old time's sake, nothing of Karen remained.

I came back out with the colored sketch of my boat, Blue Eyes. I showed it to them and they both literally gasped at the detail, color, and vibrancy of it. Simple physics prevents colored pencils from having nearly the resolution of a photograph, but there was just something about it that made you feel like you were staring straight at it. It felt like you could reach into it and touch the boat or the water.

"Eric," Frank said, trying hard to tear his eyes away from it and finally succeeding, "that girl has a gift. We're not around her as much as we'd like, but I know there's so much pure talent in her that she's going to be somebody special. You need to be careful nobody messes her up."

I nodded, blushing a little with my own selfish pride in her. "Another reason I'm happy we live about as far from civilization as you can get," I said. "Gives her a buffer from the jackals. But don't worry, I plan on being an overprotective parent every step of the way."

Susan and Frank both laughed, though Susan's seemed a little forced. Frank nodded. "I hope she doesn't need it. For what it's worth, I can't think of a better person than you for Karen to end up spending her life with." He paused before adding, "Short as it was." Frank cleared his throat and stood up. He stretched and stepped away from his chair towards the hallway to their bedroom.

"Well, it's getting late, I'm going to crash. If I know Jess, we'll need some rest if we're going to keep up with her tomorrow!"

Susan stood up slowly, sharing a smile with me at how uncomfortable Frank was at his own admission of emotions. She paused to give me a kiss on the cheek, then hesitated a moment before moving after him. I watched her curiously: had I imagined it or did she seem to want to say more? I shook my head, I was tired and probably seeing things. I tidied up my things a little bit and headed for bed myself.

I stopped at Jessica's bedroom and peered in. Susan had beaten me to it, and she straightened when she sensed me behind her. She turned and smiled, which I could make out thanks to the light filtering in from the hallway. She looked at her granddaughter again, then motioned for me to follow her out into the hall.

"Eric…" she began, then faltered and fell silent.

"What is it?" I asked her, my voice as quiet as hers. I knew she had something to tell me, something more than the earlier revelation about the phone call. Her behavior made it obvious that something was eating away at her from the inside.

"Please, you'll think I'm crazy, but hear me out," she said.

I nodded. I wanted to reassure her, but knew that it would be a foolish thing for me to say.

"My grandfather used to tell me stories when I was a little girl," she said. "He'd tell me bedtime stories when I was very young, about fantastic people and places. As I got older, the stories became more grim. They were darker and more fearsome, and they scared me."

I nodded to show I was paying attention and that nothing seemed crazy yet. After all, most childhood nursery rhymes and fairy tales had some pretty twisted themes to them.

"He told me stories about magic and fighting and all sorts of horrible things. Sacrifices and murder in the night, it was frightful," she said. "I went to my mother and asked her to please tell him to stop telling me scary stories. We lived nearby, you see, back when we lived in Vermont. She seemed a little scared herself when I told her, and she promised me not to worry about it.

"The next time my grandpa came to visit I heard my father talking to him. I heard him tell him to stop scaring me, that all those stories were just fantasies told to scare little kids. My grandpa argued. He told him they were not. Those stories were the reason my grandfather's people were there in the first place. Those stories kept people in line, he insisted, and they kept them from dabbling in things that would ruin us all.

"My dad was furious at him," she went on quickly, seeing she had not lost me but still expecting to. "He told him those were ridiculous lies.

"Grandpa shouted back. 'Magic is real', he said, 'and only by keeping women afraid of it can they be sure that none of them learns how to use it on their own. Girls can have magic in them naturally, some more than others. Men have to learn it. If any girl shows signs of it, she's burned as a witch as a lesson to the others to never think about it.' He didn't want that for me, so my dad had better keep an eye on me.

I ran away, not from my parents, just from overhearing the argument. My dad was shouting back again, but I wouldn't listen, I couldn't listen!"

She shook her head and turned to look in on Jessica again. "She's so beautiful, Eric, so beautiful and so perfect." She turned back to me. "You protect her, you hear me? You do whatever you can but you keep her safe."

I nodded, humbled by the intensity in her eyes and in her quiet but powerful voice.

"Back then, did anything else happen?" I asked her, caught up in her story even if it did seem like her grandfather was off his rocker.

"We moved away that week. All the way to California, and that's where I grew up until I met Frank," she said, her voice sounding very sad. "I never saw or talked to my grandparents again."

I gathered her up in a hug and said, "I can't help that, but I can say that you'll never have to worry about losing Jessica."

I felt her shudder as she took in a breath and got control of herself. She pulled back and nodded, smiling through the wetness in her eyes. She gave me another kiss on the cheek. "Frank's right, you know, you and Karen, you were perfect together. Whenever she and I talked she could never stop talking about you. You were the light of her life.

"I don't know anything about what I said," she added quickly. "I managed to forget all about it, in fact, until I saw that picture. It's beautiful Eric, and I mean beautiful in a way that nobody else could have done."

I realized I was nodding in agreement and stopped. I smiled and turned to look in on my daughter again. When I turned back I heard Frank grumble aloud, wondering if Susan was coming to bed. She said something about making sure I had enough blankets, then bid me goodnight and went to join him.

I went in and gave Jess a kiss on the forehead, then went to my own room to get some rest. I was exhausted, but it was a long time before sleep came to me.

Chapter 3

We spent a calm and relaxing week at the Sparks' house. As relaxed as a person can be knowing that some psychopath is trying to hunt you down, that is. Jessica handled it with the resilience of youth, and focused entirely on making each and every day not only fun for her, but a spot of sunshine for her grandparents as well.

We did the tourist thing and went out to see the sights, even traveling to Puget Sound and admiring the mountains from some scenic overlooks. Of course Jess wanted to go hiking on them, and I had to admit I felt the call as well but we held back. We didn't have the gear for such a thing. Besides that, I had to tell her the mountains here were a lot different than the ones back home. The Rockies were taller and harsher, with some cold winds and a lot of rain and snow at the upper heights. Not to mention the wildlife. Sure, we had black bears, coyotes, and wildcats, but out here they had all that and more.

Never daunted by a little thing like a grizzly bear, she only gave up when she realized that I was not going to do it, no matter what her courage or excuse. She only pouted a little, much improved over past trips when she was younger. Instead she allowed herself to focus on other things and be distracted by them.

I thought about taking a trip back up to Dutch Harbor, for old time's sake, and seeing if anybody I knew was still around. I had only lived there for about six years, and Jess for only her first two, but I figured somebody might still be there from over a decade ago that might remember me. I didn't miss the crabbing but I did have a lot of good memories of the place.

Rather than head up there though, Jess and I decided to stop putting it off and go visit Karen. We were both a little nervous, her more for me than for herself. She had never known her mom; Karen had died minutes before she was born. That upset me more than anything. All she had were stories and photos, and there is just no way to paint the complexities of a person's life and personality with words and pictures.

It was a cloudy day when we made our way to the cemetery, cloudy and wet. A typical day in Seattle, which is known for coffee, grunge music, Microsoft, and rain. We were experiencing a light mist of a rain and I figured we would deal with the grunge and the coffee later. Jess was already experiencing Microsoft on her grandparent's computer, though whether that was a good experience or not I was not sure.

At the cemetery we stood, hand in hand, and stared down at Karen's headstone. I found myself taking deep even breaths. It still felt like just yesterday I held her in my arms. I could see her sparkling blue eyes and smell the freshness of her hair when she would let me hold her close. I smiled at the memory and sighed, which made Jessica look up at me with a faint smile of her own.

She had her mother's eyes. Practically identical, the way they shone in spite of the overcast sky. Blue and irrepressible. I squeezed her hand and smiled back at her, then saw her expression change from happy to one of alarm and surprise. I spun even as Jessica's mouth opened to shout out a warning.

Johann had found us. He had emerged from behind an old-fashioned family crypt and was walking steadily towards us. Now that we knew he was there, I saw him say something and start to run towards us, his hand going into his pocket.

"Jess, run! Get to the car!" I told her, pressing my keys into her hand and pushing her away. "Go!"

I turned, trusting her to do the right thing, and ran at him, ducking low in case he pulled out another gun. Carl Lewis would have been proud, I think, because I probably crossed the hundred yards or so to him in a world record time. I tucked my head, not seeing what he now held in his hand but suspecting the worst. All I knew was that I had to buy my daughter some time, and that meant hitting him as hard as possible.

The collision drove the breath from him and made me gasp as well. Something crunched in my spine from the impact, making me feel a little funny. We were both on the ground, flailing about as I tried to get a hold of him. Realizing I was still alive and I hadn't heard a gun fire, I felt another surge of adrenaline. Instead of wanting to slow him down, I wanted to beat him into submission. I wanted to hurt him, and hurt him bad. My blood was up and I only intended one of us to walk away. That walker had to be me.

I heard him swear again, distantly, as a bolt of lightning tore through me and turned my very existence into a single moment of fiery agony. I dropped, twitching and convulsing, to the ground. My vision was a mixture of fireworks that I could not make sense of; all I could do was grit my teeth in agony. It lessened, suddenly, but my body refused to do anything but flop on the ground out of my control like I'd seen fish do on my deck, trying to get back into the safety and comfort of water.

The colors and blackness faded and I saw him struggling to his feet. He was shaken too; I wondered for a moment if the bolt of lightning had hit both of us. Feeling began to return and I ached all over. A wave of nausea ran through me and rolled over and retched onto the ground. Johann picked up something he had dropped and started staggering away from me.

Grim with determination, I forced myself to roll. I came to my hands and knees and, still not able to stand, I started to crawl after him. Within a few feet I had regained enough control to attempt to stand. I climbed up and staggered, my neurons still not firing right. I figured the object he had in his hand was a taser - only that would explain what had happened to me. I must have been touching him when he zapped me; that explained why he was in bad shape too and why my teeth felt and tasted like charcoal stumps in my mouth.

Coordination returned with each step and soon my determination overcame my body's objections. I caught him up and jumped onto his back, driving my fists into his neck in an overhand chop. He collapsed under me, the taser flying off to the side. My fists rose and fell, pounding into his back, neck, and head repeatedly while he struggled to protect himself. I never let up, knowing he only needed one chance to pull some other instrument of pain or death from concealment. I had no idea what he might have, and I knew I did not want to find out.

"Daddy! Stop!"

I heard Jessica yelling at me and, slowly, she pulled me out of the red haze of murder that had gripped me. My arms, wooden and numb, hesitated in mid-air. My chest heaved with gasps for breath. I staggered to my feet and suddenly felt as though I had not slept in a week after running a marathon.

Bile burned in my throat and my eyes ached with pressure.

"Is he…did you…"

A soft groan answered her question for both of us. I snarled, a fresh surge of anger in me. I wanted him dead. I stepped forward with one foot, the other one staying back in preparation for a crippling kick in the ribs.

"Wait," he gasped, his voice slurred. "Please!"

I waited. I should not have. I did not want to hear his words. I did not want to know him. He had killed my wife and tried to kill my daughter, he deserved the worst I could do to him, maybe more. I took a step to the side instead and picked up the taser.

"Don't move," I told him, spitting out some blood as I did so. I had bitten my tongue at some point, hard enough to draw blood.

I reached into my pocket, feeling a fresh stab of pain from my not quite healed fingers. The splint I had been wearing had come off in the struggle somewhere, and I figured they were probably broken again from the way my knuckles were beginning to ache. I tossed Jessica my phone.

"Call the cops," I growled. "And go to the car like I told you!"

Whether she listened or not I did not know, I was focusing entirely on our attacker.

"You're a lousy assassin," I muttered. "Couldn't find a rifle and a roof?"

He said nothing for a long time. I almost kicked him again. I wondered if maybe he had passed out, but then I saw him shuddering or shaking. I figured out a minute later he was crying.

"What kind of killer cries like a baby?" I asked out loud, incredulous.

He rolled over, slowly, and I saw tracks of tears running down his face. His nose was running too, all in all, he was a pathetic sight. The bruised and split lips and broken nose added to the effect.

"Please," he said again. "I'm sorry…I…I had to do it."

"Why?" I spat at him angrily. "Your mommy spank you as a child so you hate all women now?"

He turned to look at Jessica, who I realized had not left. I opened my mouth to tell her to go again, but saw her staring at him in fascination.

"She's going to get us all killed!" he said, staring at her.

The preposterous statement went unanswered. Both out of shock at his claim and because, a few seconds later, I heard the first police sirens. Jess had not placed a call, but other people in the cemetery had seen the scuffle.

"Look, you crazy son of a bitch," I growled at him. "You're going to spend the rest of your miserable life rotting in a cell. If I ever see you again, nothing is going to stop me from putting you in the ground. Nothing! You got it?"

He ignored me, just kept staring at Jessica. "So beautiful," he whispered, adding considerably to my opinion that he was a first class raving lunatic. "She's a witch," he said, looking at me and still persisting in his world of make-believe. "They'll find her and come to her! We'll all die!

"Please, you have to understand, for the best of everyone she has to die."

"Shut up!" I growled at him, wishing my daughter was not standing there so I could have hit him again. Foot, fist, taser, it did not matter, I just wanted him to shut up.

"She's already used magic! I saw the pictures! It's a beacon to the Dark Earth, they'll bridge the darkness and come for us all!" He refused to stop raving.

I opened my mouth again but was overshadowed by somebody else shouting, "Drop the weapon and get your hands up!"

I turned and saw two cops standing, pistols drawn and pointed at me. Two more were running towards us as well. I held my arms out and let the taser fall from it. Last thing I wanted was trouble with the police too. I was the good guy here!

"Little girl, come away from there," the other police officer said, trying to clear her from any danger.

"Jess, go with them," I told her, my voice calm. I smiled at her, realizing my puffy lip probably made it more of a snarl or a grimace.

"Daddy..." she said hesitantly.

"It will all work out, honey, I promise."

She nodded and let the officer lead her away. The other two had arrived by then and they moved in to search me rather briskly and cuff me. Johann received similar treatment.

"This guy peed himself!" one of them said while frisking me. He was disgusted and amused.

"Taser," I explained, blushing with humiliation. I had heard stories about taser causing that to happen. Now I could attest it was not an urban legend. Lucky me.

"I advise you not to say anything," the officer told me. He led me to one car while another cop took Johann to another. Jessica was being talked to by the officer that had gathered her up, away from both of us.

I was read my Miranda Rights and I agreed to understanding them, then sat impatiently while they sorted out the scene and asked questions of Jessica and a few bystanders who had seen what had happened and bothered to stick around. Soon they came back to me and started asking me questions.

My daughter's story and mine were the same, and matched up with the onlookers. It still looked to some of them like I had been the aggressor, but that was cleared up fairly quickly. Johann said nothing to the police, opting instead for a vow of silence. As much as I hated him, I did not blame him; the story he had to tell would sentence him to a padded room for a few dozen years, at least.

"Trying to be a hero?" one of the officers asked me, his voice communicating distaste.

"You got any kids?" I asked him. He shook his head. "Then you wouldn't understand."

He harrumphed and turned his back on me until another one came over to relieve him. Apparently this was his partner, since they were wrapping up the on scene investigation and getting ready to cart us off for questioning.

"We have to take you to the precinct for questioning," the other one said, confirming my thoughts on cue. "Sorry, but I have to leave the cuffs on until then."

Good cop, bad cop, I realized. Just what I needed, a scene out of a bad movie. "Sorry about your seat," I said to him.

He laughed. "There's been a lot worse on it!"

I looked down and frowned, which only made him laugh a little harder. "That's why they're vinyl, they get hosed down."

I nodded, it made sense. That did nothing for my sense of personal hygiene, but my options were limited. "My daughter, what are you doing with her? She's been attacked twice in a few weeks, I really don't like her being out of my sight."

He turned to look at Jessica, who had a blanket around her shoulders and was being chaperoned by another officer. “She'll go to the station too,” he said. “She mentioned her grandparents, we'll call them if your story doesn't check out. If it does, you'll get to take her with you.”

I nodded. “Thanks.”

The door swung shut, leaving me trapped in the back with no means of getting out. I was fine with it until I suddenly had a flash of paranoia. What if Johann had an accomplice? What if somebody came for her right now, while I was trapped and the police were distracted?

I craned my neck to see her and saw her being led to a third police cruiser that pulled up. She, uncuffed, was let into the back seat. I figured she was about as safe as she could be, but now I worried about some crazy running into them like Johann had done to me thirteen years ago. That and whatever else had been on the back seat of the cruiser she sat in.

I forced myself to breathe evenly and relax. She was safe. Johann was in custody. Our nightmare was almost over.

Chapter 4

"Remind me never to piss you off." The words were spoken by a woman dressed functionally in slacks, blouse, and a jacket. I suppose she was attractive enough. She had blond hair and green eyes that would sparkle when they weren't trapped under lifeless fluorescent lights. I could have cared less at the moment if she was drooling on herself, given my situation.

"I'm Detective Lauren Fargim," she told me, shutting the door behind her and sitting on the other side of the table from me. Just like in the movies, she laid a folder on the table and opened it.

"Mr. Baxter-"

"Please, detective, it's been hours. Where is my daughter?" I interrupted her, barely restraining my frustration and anger. I was exhausted, I was sore, and my mouth still tasted like an ashtray. It felt like I had a fair few burns on my cheeks and tongue from electricity arcing off my fillings.

I had long since gotten past the anxiety caused by being in a police station-and worse, being on the handcuffed side of a police station. The cuffs were gone, but the psychology they used to wear down their suspects had worked quite well on me when coupled with the mid-term debilitating effects of being electrocuted at a low amperage.

She sighed and placed her hands on the table. "She is with her grandparents. They are in our waiting room."

I breathed a little easier and even that hurt. "Okay, thank you. Now when can I get out of here?"

She nodded. "Do you realize you broke Mr. Pederson's collarbone and nose? You knocked out one tooth and chipped another. And you cracked three ribs…and dislocated his shoulder.” She read it like a laundry list that would never end.

“You don’t have any history of violence, a few dropped priors in Dutch Harbor from boys being rowdy, but that was a long time ago,” she continued. “Tell me, Mr. Baxter, why did you stop? From what our witnesses say, you were intent on beating Mr. Pederson ‘into a pulp’.”

I looked at her. Was she serious? I should have felt bad I suppose, but I didn’t. Maybe it was the aftershock of being tasered, but I was mostly numb and just wanted to get Jessica and go home. Still, her question seemed naïve, especially given her line of work. Incredulously I asked, “You realize he killed my wife, right?”

“I’m asking the questions, Mr. Baxter.”

“You see the police report from Marquette from the other day? The one where he shot my daughter?”

She gave me a look that reminded me of a stern schoolteacher and closed her folder. She stood up and said, “I’ll come back when you’re willing to answer my questions.”

“I just did answer your question!” I snapped at her. I took a moment and a few deep calming breaths. I had never had a problem with my temper before, or at least not for a long time. Something about being a single parent either teaches you tolerance or…well, I did not want to think of what the other option was. I blamed it on feeling like I just got hit by a truck.

“Look, I’m sorry, but I’ve been here a long time and I just want this to be over. I want my life to go back to normal. I want Jessica and I to go home and be able to live normal and without being afraid some psycho is going to show up and try to kill her,” I said in a rush.

She nodded and sat back down.

"Do you have any children, Detective?" I asked her, risking another question.

Apparently feeling sorry for me, she nodded. "Yes, I do. A boy and a girl."

There was no ring on her finger, I noticed. "And I thought one was rough," I said. She smirked. "What would you do if somebody came after your kids?" I asked her. "I'm not going to lie, if Jess had not been there, I probably would have killed him. All I cared about was making sure he never threatened us again. Isn't that self-defense?" I asked her.

She shrugged. "That would be up to the jury," she said. "Charging at him first looks a little suspicious."

I nodded. "Yeah, maybe, but last time I was not fast enough and she'll have a scar on the side of her head because of that."

"So why did you stop?" She came around to that first question.

I hesitated. Why had I stopped? I was running on pure adrenaline at the time, but I did not realize that until afterwards. Until the rage had left me. "Because Jessica told me to," I admitted. "She was there, and no matter how sick and evil he was, my daughter had already seen enough violence. I did not need her to see that. Besides that, I have to be better than that. For her, I mean. What kind of a role model would I be?" I added, doing some on the spot soul-searching.

"Don't watch much TV do you?" she asked. "There's plenty of violence every day on that."

I shook my head. "No TV," I told her. "No power, even. You ever been to Northern Michigan, Detective? It's not too different from driving up in the mountains around here."

She raised an eyebrow and pursed her lips. I wondered what her expressions meant. "And you're a fisherman."

"Got my own boat," I confirmed. "Whitefish mostly these days."

"They're going to have some papers for you to sign," she told me, standing back up and picking up her folder. "It's not against the law to own a taser. It is against the law to use in pursuit of a crime, however, and in this case it has been demonstrated circumstantially that he was intent upon breaking the law. Mr. Pederson will stand trial here for that, then once that is over he will head back to Michigan to stand trial for the other charges.

"He's got a lot of charges against him, and given the history of this case, I expect him to spend a lot of time behind bars. We're going to recommend a very high bail if, and that's only if, we can not convince the judge to suspend bail altogether."

"Has he said anything?" I asked her, suddenly curious. "He did a lot of babbling when I was there, but he clammed up when the police showed up. I thought I might have hit him one time in the head too many, some of the things he was saying–it didn't make any sense."

"Not a word," she confirmed. "We tried offering him an attorney and he would not even acknowledge him. He's clearly disturbed, but if he won't say anything in his defense…"

I nodded and smiled grimly. "Thank you, Detective, thank you very much."

She paused at the door then hesitated. She turned back to me and said, "Mr. Baxter, I spoke with your daughter. She's a good kid and you've done a good job raising her. You gave me the right answers, Mr. Baxter, you're free to go."

She smiled at me. She was pretty, but she looked tired and had lines on her face caused from too much stress and not enough laughter. She let me out of the room and I proceeded to the desk where I had to sign my release papers and other papers indicating I was pressing charges. Finally I had to write down and sign a statement, since I had no intention on waiting in Seattle for the days to weeks it would take before Johann went up before a judge.

My next stop was one of the happiest of my life, or at least of that week. Jessica came flying out of a chair as soon as she saw me and jumped into my arms. The aches and weakness in my body disappeared as I laughed and kissed and hugged her. I refused to put her down even when Susan hugged me and Frank shook my hand and clapped me on the shoulder repeatedly telling me I had done a great job; they were proud of me.

Recovering back at the Sparks' place felt like old times. Well, old times with residual soreness that made me wonder if I had started lifting weights in my sleep. Jessica spent a lot of time on the computer, and I wondered if she was suddenly afraid to go outside because of what had happened. I reassured Susan and Frank, when they asked, that she was just getting her technology fix in since we had almost none back at our place, but inside I worried more and more until finally I had to do something about it.

"Hey kid," I said to her on our third day. She gave me a look that reminded me how much she detested it when I called her 'kid'. "Want to go for a walk or something? It's not raining out–I figure we've got a good twenty minutes before the next shower hits."

She glanced at the computer then shrugged and mumbled "OK". She shut it down and we headed out. The sky was overcast, but the blue in the West promised a beautiful sunset that evening. We walked silently side by side down the sidewalk for a while, her staring mostly at the sidewalk while I would look at her and around. Gone was my urge to keep glancing over my shoulder.

"Hey," I said, surprised. She glanced up at me inquiringly. "I just realized I'm not staring into every dark corner anymore," I said, hoping to make her open up. I was admitting my own revelation too, so I was being honest too.

She nodded, but then looked away.

"Jess, what's wrong?" I asked her after a few more silent steps. The sun broke through the clouds almost as if it was a sign, warming us with its radiance.

She sighed and looked up at me. The look in her eyes took the warmth out of the sunshine. Almost like it was another omen, another cloud slipped between it and us. We were cast in shadow as she spoke. "Dad, what that creep said…about me…"

"Honey, he was-"

"I wasn't done," she said, interrupting my interruption. "You want me to talk, let me talk."

I bit my lip to keep from laughing at the remonstration. "I'm sorry," I said, "please continue."

She nodded. "What did he mean, do you think?"

I hesitated before answering, and rightly so because it looked like the question was rhetorical. "I've been using grandpa and grandma's computer to try and find something about the stuff he talked about. I didn't find much of anything…it doesn't make sense. Why me? Why mom? Why come after us at all?"

I waited while she lapsed into expectant silence. "You can talk now," she said softly after a moment.

I took her hand in mine.

"Jess, I don't know any more about what he said than you do. I wish I could tell you why 'us'." I paused and smiled at her reassuringly. "There's a lot of things I don't understand. I'm just some guy with a boat that can catch fish for a living. You're the special one here, you're the one who's supposed to take the world by gills and have it all figured out."

She made a face at my expression but even that failed to cheer her up. "Why me?" she asked. "Why do I have to do all that? There's nothing wrong with what you do or who you are, don't make it sound like there is!"

I raised an eyebrow, surprised at her response. She was right, there was nothing wrong with it, it kept us fed and we lived a pretty comfortable life. I had a lot of luck and skill at finding the fish so we never went hungry.

"There's nothing wrong with it," I agreed with her. "It's just that I'm your father. I want a better life for you. I want you to have everything you ever dreamed of. I don't imagine cleaning fish ranks too high on your list of childhood dreams."

She wrinkled her nose again at the thought. "Fish stink," she admitted, and I laughed. She laughed with me after a moment and I felt the sunshine was back on us even if the clouds were still in the way.

"I'm scared, daddy," she said softly, her hand squeezing mine.

I squeezed back. "Hey, we stopped him this time. There's no way he's getting out now, not for a long, long time."

"All the stuff I looked up, there are a lot of crazy people that think the end of the world is coming," she said. "What if he was in some cult and there are more of them?"

If nothing else, I was glad we had no computer at home–a few days on one and this was what she had used it for. The thought had crossed my mind too, given what Susan had told me. It seemed too crazy to entertain, but now that she mentioned it, I wondered if I would have trouble sleeping because of it. I hid that though, or tried to, and instead I just smiled at her.

"Hey, we stopped this guy, didn't we? We can do it again."

Jessica's hand trembled a little in mine and she said in a soft voice, "I don't know anything about magic; I can't be a witch!"

"There's no such thing as magic, sweety," I told her in the calmest voice I had. "You're a very special girl, that's all. You've got more talent in your little finger than most people do in their entire lives."

"I don't want to be special," she pouted. "I want to be normal!"

It was the closest to a tantrum I had seen her throw in about ten years. It was almost cute, but at the same time it was breaking my heart to hear her say such things, even if I knew she did not mean them. I pulled her to me, overcoming her initial resistance until she clung to me and began to sob.

"Jess," I whispered once the worst of her sobs had died off. "We can't change the past. Let's just make the best of what happened, learn from it, and move on. I expect you'll become whatever you want and make my life difficult every step of the way. And you know what?"

"Everything's going to be all right?" she asked in a tone that I knew was always coupled with her rolling her eyes. "That's what you always say."

"And I'm sure it will," I said, hiding my amusement. I guess I did overuse the phrase if my thirteen year old was telling me as much. "But that wasn't what I was going to say."

She looked up at me, surprised and willing to humor me. "What?"

"I'll love you more and more for it," I said, smiling to know I had managed to keep one step ahead of her. It was getting harder with every year older she grew.

She smiled back in spite of herself, burying her face in my chest. I heard a muffled, "I love you daddy."

"One more thing," I said to her, which made her step back from me. I could see the suspicious look in her eyes; she expected my catch phrase this time. I was only too happy to disappoint her. "I promise to let you know any time I think you're acting like a witch."

Her jaw dropped, shocked that I would say such a thing. The grin on my face lasted all the way back to Frank and Susan's house, including the first dozen feet that she chased me until I let her catch me and slap me playfully on the arm.

Chapter 5

We left the next morning, driving back home after a tearful farewell with Frank and Susan. I reassured them we would be back in a couple of months for the usual holiday routine, and that made them feel better. Neither Jess nor I really wanted to leave, but I was afraid Susan's cooking would keep my clothes from fitting comfortably for a few weeks. The woman had a fondness for baking cookies and sweets and she saw to it that we brought several tins home full of goodies. Between that and knowing that I had responsibilities to my boat and crew, as well as making sure my daughter went to school, made the decision less difficult for me.

Once something happens to you, you are forever changed by it. As Fall left us and Winter came and went, the thought of a cult of crazy people that considered Jessica to be the Anti-Christ plagued me. In our case, most especially mine, every time I saw an unfamiliar face looking in her direction, I wondered if it was chance or if there was more to it. My first trip back out on the Blue Eyes was torture for me. It was everything I could do to not cut it short and return with a hold only half full. As it was I made Jessica stay with Jake's wife and kids while we were out. Surprisingly, for her, she had not protested.

Jess had been staying on her own for about a year before Johann showed up. There are probably a lot of parents out there who'd still think a thirteen year old isn't old enough, but they didn't know my kid. I'd even had a police officer tell me my kid was something special now, what more proof did I need?

In spite of that, I was not ready to risk it again. Not out of fear for what she might do, but rather what might be done to her. What Johann had done was so out there, so crazy and outlandish, that I could not help but wonder if there might be more people like him. Hearing Susan's childhood story and then the babblings of Johann had opened my eyes to a world of madness.

In spite of my new found paranoia, things did slowly return to normal for us. Jessica put it behind her more easily than I did but she never gave me a hard time when I showed signs of being overly protective. She busied herself with her artwork, drawing and painting and experimenting with various other styles.

The months wore on and we returned to Seattle to visit her grandparents for the holidays. It was a good time, filled with a lot of laughter and family. Every year I ached at how Karen was not there to enjoy it, but this time around after what had happened to us, I thought about her a little less and more about those of us that were there. I might have even been taking my own advice: letting the past go in order to make the best out of the present.

Winter turned into Spring and the ice broke free a little early. I knew I would miss the extra time Jess and I spent together most winters when I could not get my boat out, but I was also glad to give her some room to breathe and grow on her own too. I was no less protective, but I understood her need to experience things on her own. Besides, I was looking forward to coming home and seeing what new artistic creation she had produced.

It turned out to be, of all things, gardening. She excitedly told me how she had cleared the weeds out of a clearing on our property, broken up the ground on her own with a rake and a hoe, and then talked Mrs. Tenyke into taking her to the store so she could buy a bunch of seeds for it. I always left her money when I went out, in case she needed anything, and in spite of my first thoughts of disapproval I told myself to hold my tongue until I saw what she had done. Somehow I knew I would not be disappointed.

She took me through the trees, some just beginning to show buds on their branches. We passed over a stream-a small trickle really-that fed into the Wilson Creek a few miles away. There was some new logs across it, lashed together with twine. I chuckled, realizing I was going to have to redo the makeshift bridge and make it properly if it was going to hold up beyond a few weeks. Across the creek and over a small hill we went into the clearing she had been working on. I was impressed immediately, as I'd known I would be.

She had, by hand, tilled about an acre's worth of ground. While that was impressive enough to start with, even more so was the fact that seedlings of the various plants she had sewn were already breaking free of the ground. I stared in shock at it, and had to ask her again to verify that she had planted seeds, not seedlings.

"The ground is really fertile here, daddy," she explained to me as though that told me everything I would ever need to know.

Fertile ground? Maybe, but there was no ground anywhere that fertile. I shook my head, figuring the seeds must have already been starting to germinate. I moved on to the next question then, which was my way of playing Devil's Advocate to see if Jessica really had thought everything through.

"It's a lot of ground to protect, honey," I told her. "It's going to take some time to put up a fence around it to keep the animals out."

She just grinned at me. "Don't worry, I had a talk with them, they'll leave it alone."

She had me staring at her stupidly again. "You had a talk with them?"

She nodded. "I told them if they left it alone then when I harvested I would leave some for them. It will be when they need it too, near the Fall so they can fatten up for Winter."

"And they agreed to this?" I asked, humoring her because, honestly, I had no idea what else to do.

She nodded again. "I think the rabbit was doubtful," she said thoughtfully, "but he's going to give it a shot and see."

"And just how many of these animals did you talk to?" I was growing amused at her imagination, but it also made me wonder if maybe she needed to spend more time around others her own age. Preschoolers held conversations with animals, not teenagers. I wondered if the recent events had caused some sort of regression.

She ticked off her fingers as she counted in her head. "Let's see, there were three squirrels, a rabbit, two porcupines–they were so cute together–a momma deer and two fawns, and a muskrat. Don't worry though," she said before I could interrupt, "I told them to make sure they told the other animals about the deal."

Rather than have her think I considered her crazy, I turned and stared at the large garden. Something seemed peculiar about it, so rather than dwell on the unlikely conversation with animals, I moved closer to the garden and studied it. The way she had planted the various crops was not in straight rows, but rather in odd designs that made no sense to me.

"Why didn't you plant it in rows?" I asked her.

She shrugged. "This just made more sense to me," she explained. "More wind, sun, and rain can get to them, and they can have more ground for their roots to spread too."

There were patterns to it, I realized, patterns that reminded me of some of her artwork. I walked around the edge, staring at it and just letting myself be amazed. I stopped trying to figure it out finally and just shrugged. It was on my way back to a smiling Jessica that I noticed something else: there were paw prints of different animals around the edge of the garden, but not a single one crossed over the edge and into it. I tried to dismiss it as old prints that she had not tilled but many of them were on the tilled earth at the edges that she had not planted.

"Well, you like?" she asked me when I got back to her.

I nodded and stared at her in amazement. "Sweety, you're something else."

Unbidden and unwanted, the memory of last Fall's conversation entered my mind. Plants do not grow that fast, not on their own or with the best of fertilizer, water, and lights. Or at least none that I had ever heard of. I took comfort in my ignorance; I was just a small time fisherman trying to make a living on the fringes of civilization. The alternative to me being ignorant meant the impossible. And with the impossible came even scarier thoughts. Thoughts that involved cults of murderous crazy people.

She grinned widely, proud of herself and happy to have gotten my approval. She hugged me and I hugged her back, but all the time my head was swimming with the peculiarity of what I had seen; a whirlpool of terror threatening to suck me in.

We went back to the house and I told her that I would help fix up the bridge over the weekend before I went out on my next fishing trip. She was excited at the prospect of helping, and I took in her buoyant happiness and used it to remind myself that magic was not real. She just had a green thumb and everything was going to be okay.

I was nearly chanting my mantra as I was drifting off to sleep that night. My relative peace was shattered when I heard a wolf howl. It was not unheard of up there, just unusual. We had wolves and moose, though they usually stayed further to the West towards the Porcupine mountains. This one sounded close, though. Not right outdoors close, but still nearby.

I heard footsteps running across the floor downstairs and then on the stairs. A few moments later Jess jumped into my bed.

"Did you hear the wolf, daddy?"

I nodded, smiling to show her it was all right. She relaxed a little, but I could still see how tense she was. "You won't let him get me, right?"

I wanted to laugh at the ridiculous question, but something about her tense posture kept me from doing so. "Don't worry, sweety, no wolf stands a chance of getting past me."

She smiled and hugged me, then burrowed in and slipped under the covers. Before I knew it she looked up at me and begged with her eyes while asking, "Can I sleep with you tonight? Please?"

I sighed. She was thirteen and I was somehow still her best friend. I decided she really did need to spend more time with kids her age-too much time at home, as much as I enjoyed it, was turning her into a recluse.

"Just tonight, dad, don't worry," she said, as though she could read my mind. Her tone was just right too, making me laugh at myself for what now seemed to be silly worries.

"All right, but just tonight."

* * * *

The next day, after breakfast, we went out to work on the bridge. I figured we would do it right so we drove off to the lumberyard off US-41 and picked up the supplies I figured we would need. Jessica found a woodcarving set that excited her, so that ended up in the bed of my truck as well. I could only imagine what she would create with this latest hobby.

The stream was about a hundred yards from the house, through some trees that were thankfully free of undergrowth. That was the great thing about most of the forests where we lived: unless it was swampy, there was next to no undergrowth. Just tall beautiful trees that could stand the harsh winters and shorter summers, including a fair amount of evergreens where the hardwoods gave them room to grow and feel the sun.

Needless to say, it was still going to be a lot of trips carrying wood back and forth, especially considering I had no intention of hauling my generator and table saw all the way over to it. I sighed at the labor ahead of me and made plans with Jessica on how we were going to go about it. We started by heading to the stream to find the best spot and take some measurements.

We figured out what we wanted and I took the necessary measurements before I stood up and looked around. Something felt different. I had a flashback to when Johann had attacked Jessica, and I turned quickly to see her picking a pretty stone that had been smoothed by years of water flow out of the stream. She was safe, but something was still wrong.

"Where are the birds? The squirrels? Even the mosquitoes?" I asked rhetorically.

Jessica looked around, alerted to their absence now that I had mentioned it. "The wolf!" she said, gasping.

I turned, looking around but not seeing it. "A wolf?" I asked her once I was sure it was not breathing down our necks. "A wolf is an animal, honey, it would not scare away the rest of the animals."

She shook her head. "This one did," she said. "It's a bad wolf."

"A bad wolf?" I asked her, wondering what that meant or how she could know.

"Dad, I'm not a little kid, you know," she said to me reproachfully. "I know a lot more than you think I do."

I chuckled, in spite of my worry. "I know, honey, I just don't understand how you know it's a bad wolf or why you think it scared away the other animals."

"Didn't you hear it last night?" she asked me.

I nodded.

"No, I mean did you really hear it?"

I cocked my head. "I heard it howl, I've heard wolves do that before, just a wolf howling at the moon."

She shook her head. "Nuh-uh," she said. "He's angry and he's looking for something. It wasn't sad or lonely or hungry, he's up to no good."

"You could tell that from a howl?" I asked her, partially humoring her and partially wondering if I was losing my sanity. Then again, maybe she was losing hers.

She nodded. "I know you don't always believe me, but you try and you want me to feel good," she said to me, surprising me with not only her words, but her seriousness and her expression. She was not chastising me, but she was letting me know in a way that made my heart ache for her. I could only feel sadness at how she was trying to be a little girl for herself and for me, but it was almost impossible for her because of what she had been through and things that she had seen and done. "Daddy, I don't know how these things happen, but they are real. I'm not imagining them. I could feel that in the wolf's howl, just like I could feel that the animals heard me the other day about staying out of my garden."

I nodded. I found myself believing her even though even bit of common sense and practicality I had in me told me she was off her rocker.

"All right, well, stay with me today, okay?" I told her. "No wandering off, just in case..."

"Just in case I'm right and that wolf is pissed off?" I frowned at her. She rolled her eyes at me and said, "Come on dad, it's not that bad of a word. I'm a teenager now, I'm supposed to be like that."

My scowl said it all. "Do you hear me swearing very often?" I asked her.

She sighed and shook her head. "Almost never," she admitted.

"All right then," I told her. "If an adult can manage to speak with respect and civility, I expect you to be able to do it too. Besides, I'm not just an adult, I'm a sailor!"

My smile was infectious, apparently, because she brightened a moment later, apologized, and then we were back to working on the bridge. Our next trip back to the house had me stepping into the house to remove a pistol from my gun safe, though. I had picked it up after last year's troubles. I told the clerk in the store I wanted the best chance at stopping someone in a home defense situation and he had immediately recommended the beast I buckled around my belt. He said he guaranteed it to stop a bear at short range, let alone a man. It was a Desert Eagle .50 caliber semi-automatic pistol. I had fired it a few times and was impressed with the kick it had and the damage it did to the targets I had set up.

In spite of the unnatural stillness of the forest we managed to get the bridge built in a single day. There was nothing special to it, just several boards screwed into three vertical struts spanning the narrow stream. Some additional bracing between the struts ensured it would last a few years, at least, and some posts cemented into holes on either end would keep it in place. We finished pretty late, and since the Spring was only just on us, it was getting chilly in spite of our jackets as the sun threatened to dip below the trees.

"Let's head back," I told her, picking up my cordless screwdriver and the box of screws.

"Wait, daddy," she said. "I want to check my garden first."

"We were just there yesterday," I reminded her.

She shrugged and I found myself following her over the new bridge and then the hill beyond it. We stopped and stared, stunned by the sight of it.

Instead of the lush growth I had almost been expecting, what we saw was even more impossible. The garden was as vibrant and filled with new life as it had been the previous day; however, the dirt around it was torn up as though something had tried desperately to get inside but had been unable to do so. We hurried down to it, my eyes shooting to the trees to look for some sign of who or what could have caused the damage that had been done.

On all sides of the garden the earth was shredded and broken. In some places piles of dirt had amassed, in others trenches. Jessica gasped and I came to her side in time to see the bloody carcass of a deer laying in a shallow rut. It was one of the spotted fawns she had mentioned. Elsewhere we saw other bodies of animals, all of them not only dead, but torn apart as though they had been set upon by a malevolent piece of farm machinery.

"Jess, back to the house," I told her, even as she bent down to pick up the body of a squirrel that seemed physically unharmed, yet was still stiff and dead. "Now!"

She hurried back with me, my eyes still searching everywhere. The sun, almost on cue, dipped below the trees just as we left the clearing behind. We had enough light to get back but I was more paranoid than ever as I tried to pierce the deepening gloom of the forest looking for shadowy attackers. We made it to the house without a problem.

I set the drill and the screws on the kitchen counter and took a deep breath. Jessica was huddled over the squirrel, her shoulder shaking as she sobbed and her tears running down her face to drop on the dead animal. I shook my head and wondered what I had done to deserve whatever punishment was being given to her.

I checked the pistol at my side, making sure it was where it should be. It had felt awkward earlier, having it holstered there, but now I was accustomed to its weight. I glanced outside and, on an impulse, locked the door.

A gasp made me spin back to Jess. I looked around, seeing her not staring outside but rather into the dead critter in her hands. I looked up just in time to see a dark shape hurtling towards the door. It slammed into it, making Jessica scream and me jump a little in surprise. The door held, but whatever was out there hit it again. I heard the cracking of wood and I knew the door would not hold.

"Upstairs!" I shouted at her, backing up some but stepping in front of the door and drawing my pistol. She ran to the stairs and flew up them, and I heard her dive under my bed once she got there. The sound of her hitting the floor coincided with the third, decisive strike against the door. The deadbolt tore free of the jamb, taking a chunk of wood with it, and the door slammed open to reveal the largest wolf I had ever seen.

I pulled the trigger but felt it resist. The safety! I had forgotten to take the safety off in my excitement. I flicked it and squeezed the trigger again as the wolf lunged at me. Not only was it huge but, just as Jessica had told me, it was clearly very angry. Its fur was mottled silver and black, and it had a blue eye and a brown one. Half-unconsciously I noticed these things-those and how large its jaw was and sharp its teeth looked. I pulled the trigger two more times.

Each firing of the cannon in my hands was like hitting my eardrums with a sledgehammer. In the house the sound the .50 caliber handgun made was well on the other side of deafening. The pistol leapt in my hands with each shot too, guaranteeing I would have trouble hitting the broadside of a barn even if I had been inside it.

The first bullet missed, and tore up a large chunk of my hardwood floor. The second one I thought hit the wolf; hair flew off its flank. It seemed the bullet only grazed it though, and caused it to duck under the third one before it slammed into me.

I could hear nothing but a dull ringing, so I had no idea what noise I made as I crashed to the ground with a wolf atop me. The handgun fell out of my hand as I tried to fend the wolf off, but I managed to lodge my forearm in the back of its mouth to keep the jaws from snapping on my neck. My other arm I wrapped around it, keeping it close to me to prevent it from getting its mouth free and snapping it shut on my head. As it was the pain in my arm was excruciating, but my sturdy denim Carhartt jacket kept the teeth from piercing my skin. Instead the wolf just crushed my arm with its teeth.

I knew I was a dead man when I felt one of the wolf's hind legs kick up and try to rip my belly as it thrust backwards. My belt and jeans saved me the first time, but I knew I would tire out long before the wolf did. I let go of him even as he tried again and managed to tear some great furrows on the inside of my right thigh all the way to the knee. I felt it, but the pain was a distant thing. Adrenaline was doing its job again. My hand grabbed the pistol and I shoved the barrel into the side of the wolf's thick chest and pulled the trigger.

One handed, the gun kicked even worse and made me wonder if my wrist had just been broken by it. The wolf yelped and jumped away from me, yanking me off balance and spinning me on the floor until it whipped its head back and forth and tore its jaw free of my arm. It backed away even as I struggled to bring the gun around to aim at it again. I saw it turn its head, nostrils flaring as it sniffed, and it looked up to the loft. It turned back to look at me and licked its lips, then, with a final growl, it turned and bolted through the door. I tried to rise up and go after it, or at least get another shot off at it, but my leg made its injury known to me as I attempted to use the shredded muscle in my thigh.

I managed to crawl over and shut the door, at least, and I rested there against it, breathing heavily and staring around dazed. I set the pistol down beside me and put a hand on my leg, putting pressure against it even though surprisingly little blood seeped from it.

Before my hearing had returned and before I could even really begin to try and think straight, I saw Jessica enter my field of vision. She was there, in front of me. I reached out for her with my other hand, happy to see her and wanting to hold her close to me at the same time I wanted to hide her away from whatever was after her. She came to me and hugged me, wetting my chest with her tears. I tucked one arm around her, holding her closely. I could still hear nothing but the ringing noise, though it was slowly fading and I thought I might be able to hear something muffled in the distance.

She pulled away from me and pulled her ponytail back away from her face. With a look of serious concentration, she reached over to my leg and pulled my hand away. I resisted at first, but she insisted, and eventually I let her win. I did not want her to see me hurt. Anybody, really, but especially not her own father. I was supposed to be invincible; the man all other men would be judged against.

I grinned at my own stupid thoughts and then realized I was probably going into shock. Why else would I be so lethargic and disoriented?

My hearing came back with a sudden clarity that was every bit as deafening as the pistol shots had been. I heard her sniffing, my own labored breathing, the wind blowing against the trees and the house, the fire crackling in my wood stove, and even my own heart beating. For a second I thought I could hear her heart beating too.

"Daddy, get up, you need to rest," she told me, circles under her eyes as she turned to look at me.

I nodded, even though I knew sleep was the last thing I could afford. If I slept the wolf might return. It wanted her, I knew that now. It was crazy and impossible, but I knew it beyond any doubt. As surely as Johann had tried to claim her, so did the wolf. I was just an obstacle in the way.

"It wants you, honey. We have to get away. Far away," I told her.

"Daddy, you shot it," she reminded me.

I nodded. I had shot it. Shot it right in the chest with a really big gun. My hand slipped down to the gun and I lifted it up to look at it. "I did," I said.

"Come on, you're too big," she said, pulling on my other hand.

I nodded again and used my good leg to rise to my feet. I was off balance and a little nauseous , but I found I could bear weight on my shredded leg as well. It was weak, but it worked. I was unable to think, so I just let her lead me to the stairs. The stairs were a challenge, but I tackled them with a single minded effort that seemed Herculean at the time. Jess squeaked and rushed past me right before I collapsed onto my bed. She grabbed something from it, then came to me and helped me get situated. She kissed me on the cheek and told me to rest, that she'd be right there. That was the last I knew.

Chapter 6

I woke up feeling ravenously hungry. My stomach growled and I instantly picked up the scent of coffee coming from downstairs. Everything came back to me in a rush and I gasped. My stomach clenched and I sat up quickly, worried and ashamed. How could I have left Jessica alone and unguarded all night? The smells of breakfast calmed my racing heart, but did nothing to save me from feeling like a failure as a dad.

I threw the covers back and rolled out of bed. My leg was stiff but I did not give it much thought until I was down the stairs and staring at my daughter. She was looking up at me from where she was stacking the wood stove. On the arm of the couch a few feet away a squirrel looked at me, his whiskers quivering as he sniffed the air. I stared, momentarily lost. The neurons had stopped firing, I think, because nothing made sense.

I looked down, saw the shredded mess my jeans had become and noticed in particular how my blood had dried and crusted on them. My leg was a mess, why was I walking on it? I looked back at her and saw her shut the stove door then straighten up. The squirrel chattered from his perch, drawing my attention.

"Wha…why is there a squirrel in the house?" I asked, focusing on the only thing that I could make sense of.

"Sit down, daddy, you're not going to believe any of this," she told me with a weak smile.

I nodded. I believed her already. I knew I would continue to believe her no matter how crazy it seemed. "Just a minute," I said, and I headed to the door so I could go out to the bathroom.

She had pushed a chair against the door to hold it shut. The lock and hitch for the knob had been torn out by the wolf last night. I pulled it away and made my way out to the toilet, where I did my business and then paused long enough to look at my leg with my jeans out of the way. Instead of torn flesh what awaited my eyes was three angry red lines of scar tissue. They looked jagged and freshly healed; it was impossible.

I walked back in and collapsed on the couch. The squirrel had moved to the driftwood coffee table sitting a few feet away. He chattered at me, but as I did not speak squirrel language, I had no idea what he was going on about. Jessica brought me a cup of coffee and sat down in a chair nearby.

"This is Percy," she said, gesturing to the squirrel.

I raised my cup in a greeting to the squirrel then took a drink. It was hot, but it tasted good so I did not care if it scorched all the way down.

"Daddy, Percy was the squirrel I brought in yesterday from the garden."

I set my cup down on the coffee table and sighed. Percy walked over and sniffed at it, then backed away and returned to his two legged posture. "Huh?"

She looked tired herself, like she had not slept for a while. She also looked like she was ready to cry even though she was smiling. "I don't know."

"Wasn't he dead?" I asked her.

"Stiff as a board," she said.

I shook my head. "I don't understand-"

"You think I do? Daddy, I'm not making this up!"

I held up my hand to silence her. "I don't understand," I said again. "It's not possible, but I believe you. Just like it's not possible for my leg to be almost healed this morning, but it is. Honey…I hate to say this, but I think that wack-o was right." Her eyes widened and her face paled. "No!" I said quickly. "Not that you're a danger and that you need to die! Never that honey, I promise! I mean about the magic. I mean…I don't know what I mean," I sighed and reached for my cup again. After another sip I said, "There's just no other explanation." My thoughts returned to the previous night, to the wolf."That was a strong wolf," I said. "I didn't see him when I went out there, he must have limped into the woods before he died."

"He's not dead," she half-whispered.

"Not dead? He has to be! I shot him in the chest with the biggest gun this side of the Mackinaw Bridge! You didn't see him again, did you?" I asked her, suddenly worried.

She shook her head. "No, but daddy, I looked in here and outside a little this morning. You shot him, I saw it–but there was no blood. He didn't get hurt, you just scared him off."

"Not hurt?" I repeated. "You've seen what that gun does." I trailed off, feeling overwhelmed in spite of my strange energy and how good my body felt.

Speaking of the gun, I had left it upstairs on the table next to my bed. I almost got up to go and get it, but I stopped, realizing it apparently did me no good. I took another drink and looked to her. "What now?"

She shrugged, smiling apologetically.

"So there's this thing that looks like a wolf after you that I can't stop," I said, recapping the worst of it. "Oh, and this little thing about you bringing dead squirrels back to life and helping old men walk again."

That made her smile in spite of our situation. Percy chattered indignantly. Well, it sounded indignant to me.

"We need a computer," she said.

I blinked at the apparent change of subject. "Why?"

"The Internet!"

I stared at her blankly. Computers were not my thing. I still paid my bills with cash and checks. Old fashioned I guess. Besides, the last time she'd used a computer, she had gotten herself worked up into thinking a cult of comet-worshippers were trying to kill her.

"Dad! Come on, you know what that is," she said, sounding exasperated. I nodded. Of course I knew about the Internet. Mostly I thought of it as another way that technology was making people fat, anti-social, and forgetful of just how beautiful the outdoors really was. "We can use it to learn all sorts of things. What I can do, what that wolf really is, stuff like that!"

I shrugged. "Okay, well, we don't have power here, remember? And the last time you tried you had no luck at all, you just got both of us worked up."

"Both of us?" she asked, a little surprised.

"Yeah, both of us," I told her, then took another drink.

She stared at Percy a long minute then brightened up and said, "The library!"

"Books?" I asked, confused. "I thought you wanted a computer."

She squealed in frustration. "You know I love you, daddy," she said to me a moment later. "But sometimes you're just so…so…so old!"

I smiled in spite of myself. I certainly was not feeling old, although by all rights I should have been in a pine box or at any rate the hospital.

"They have computers with free access to the Internet at the library!" she explained.

"Oh," I said, educated by my daughter, not for the first time. I shrugged. "I guess we can start there then. No cults though, I think we've got enough to worry about."

The sound of tires crunching through the sand and rocks on the road made me snap my head around. A few seconds later I saw a vehicle, this one an old Cadillac, pull into my driveway and park beside my truck. It was not a car I had seen before, nor did I recognize the gray haired man that got out of it.

"Honey, go to the root cellar," I told her. I had no feeling one way or another about the visitor, but I was concerned. Too many things had happened recently for this unknown visitor to be a coincidence.

She gave me a look but saw that I had no intention of changing my mind. Scooping Percy up, she hurried over and threw back a rug we had covering a trap door. She pulled it up and climbed down the stairs, pulling the door shut behind her only after she turned on the rechargeable electric lantern we stored down there. I arranged the rug and then went to the door, beating him to it by only a few seconds.

He reached up to knock but paused when he saw me through the window in the door. He smiled and said, "Mr. Baxter?"

"I am, who are you and what do you want?" Normally I am a little more polite to guests, even the uninvited ones that knock rather than barging in with fangs bared. He caught me at a bad time.

"Jerry Scholz," he claimed. "I want to talk to you about Mr. Pederson."

"You his attorney?" I asked, eyes narrowing. I resisted the urge to look at the trap door; it was better I gave nothing away. I did wish I had not left my gun on the bedside table.

"No, I'm an associate of his," he said, frowning. "I understand if-"

"If I want you to get off my property right now before I call the police?" I finished for him, growing angry.

He smiled, not in a haughty way, but with understanding. "Well yes, that too. I know how you must feel, Eric, but I really must speak with you. Your daughter's life is at danger. Indeed, all of us are at risk."

I stared at him for a long moment, thinking. Had the wolf never showed up, I would have happily introduced my foot to his butt and sent him on his way. Now though, after last night...

"Go back to your car and sit in the back seat," I told him. "Make sure I can see you, and don't even think about moving until you see me open the door and motion you to come in, got it?"

He raised an eyebrow but nodded. He turned and headed back to his car. As soon as he got in, I bolted upstairs, grabbing my pistol and then hurrying back downstairs. I checked to make sure he was in his car-he wasand then I unlocked my gun safe and took out the box of ammunition for the pistol. After I reloaded I went to the door, gun in plain sight in my hand at my side, and moved the chair so I could open the door. I waved him in.

My gun pointed in his direction, though not directly at him, I waved him to the couch and sat in the chair Jessica had been in earlier. My stomach grumbled but I ignored it. Half a cup of coffee was hardly enough to hold me over.

"All right, talk," I told him.

"What happened to your door?" he asked. He had noticed it right away after coming in and he seemed both preoccupied and alarmed by it.

"Been meaning to fix that," I lied.

He stared at it for a long moment then turned to look at me. "Mr. Baxter…may I call you Eric?"

"Only if it helps you get to your point faster," I told him rudely.

He smiled. "Very well. Eric, what happened was very unfortunate and I am terribly sorry about it. Johann was always a little too extreme."

"Too extreme?" I interrupted, amazed at his arrogance. "He killed my wife and very nearly finished off both myself and my unborn daughter! Then, if that was not extreme enough, he found us here and put a gun to my daughter's head! He tried to kill her! Yeah, that's a little too extreme," I said. "What sick organization are you from where you could possibly consider that only a little excessive?"

He nodded and glanced away uncomfortably. "We've had to do it so many times," he said softly. "I don't expect you to believe me, but it breaks my heart every time. My role in life is not for the faint of heart," he continued before my stunned outrage could turn into something ugly. "When my time comes and I face my maker, I have only my beliefs that I did the best that I could for everyone to support me. The blood of so many innocents will stain my soul though…I expect to face an eternity of darkness." He looked at me, a strange energy in his eyes. "I accept that, Eric, because it is people like myself that ensure that people like you can live their life as they want to."

"I would have wanted to live my life with my entire family," I snapped at him.

He nodded. "Yes, well, point taken. Perhaps not you then, but everyone else," he held up his hand to forestall any further outbursts from me. "We're getting off track, and I am confusing you, I'm sure. Johann went too far. He was not authorized to do what he did, he has been out of touch with us since his incarceration ended."

"Who are you?" I asked him, growing tired of how complicated things were becoming.

"Let me ask you something first, Eric," he said, looking around the room. His eyes centered on the drawing of Blue Eyes that Jessica had drawn for me before our world had been turned upside down. He nodded and muttered, "Yes, it's true," then turned his attention back to me. "Have you witnessed your daughter doing anything amazing? Not simple things, but truly impossible things that defy explanation?"

I realized I was nodding before I could think my answer through properly. Scowling at my own mistake, I said, "She's a talented girl, good at everything she does."

I heard Percy chitter from the root cellar beneath us, just faintly. Jerry looked around, surprised to hear a squirrel from inside, but then returned his attention to me.

"Yes, I can see she is quite artistic," he said, glancing to the picture again. "That's not enough though, and that is good.

"Mr. Baxter, I am known as the High Warden, and believe it or not, you and I have something in common."

I snorted derisively.

"Oh, I don't expect you to believe me, but I'll prove it soon enough. To be a warden means to be a protector. Over the years I have risen to be the High Warden, protector of Earth."

I laughed at that. He looked annoyed so I said, "Sorry, I didn't recognize you without your cape and tights."

"Oh, I assure you, I am every bit as mortal as you are, Eric, there are no super-powers I possess."

He glanced at my jeans, something I wondered about since it was obvious I had been recently injured and he had not yet inquired about it. "Or perhaps I am less mortal than you–tell me, what happened to you? Your leg, your arm, the door."

I shrugged. "Lots of animals up here, some of them are big and ornery, especially when they're hungry or caught up in a trap."

He nodded. "I don't doubt that, but I do doubt that happened to you. Please, tell me what happened. You walk as though you are fine, but you bear the signs of having been very recently been injured."

"Just scratches," I muttered. "Looks worse than it was."

The root cellar door flew open then, making me jump a little and causing Jerry to spin around in surprise. Jessica thrust her head up through It, an expression on her face that showed she was clearly annoyed. She looked cute, but I expected I was the target of her foul mood.

"Daddy! Tell him what happened!" she snapped at me, coming to stand with her arms crossed. Behind her the squirrel climbed up out of the cellar and ran across the floor to stand on its own hind legs beside her.

"Jess-"

"I know, dad," she said, cutting me off. "He's not like the other guy…I can tell."

"What about, you know, last night..."

"He's not like the wolf either," she said, glaring at me.

Jerry stood up, surprised. "The wolf?" He asked, looking from Jessica to me and then at my arm and leg in particular. "A wolf did that to you?"

I looked at him for a long minute, then nodded. "Big wolf," I added. "I shot him, but he got away."

He muttered something I did not understand. It was not English, whatever it was he had said. He looked back up at us and stood up. "Please, sit together. We have much to discuss and I fear little time to do it."

Jessica came over and I gathered her protectively against me. We sat on the couch together, her curling up into my side, while Jerry took the recently vacated chair.

"You shot him but he got away? What happened?"

I sighed and told him the story, starting with Jessica's garden being surrounded by torn up ground and the carcasses of many animals. Percy squeaked at this, as though he understood what I was saying, and burrowed under Jessica's leg on the couch, which she had drawn up.

"There was no blood, you are sure?" he asked after I finished. I nodded. "You need silver bullets," he said absent-mindedly. "Or something enchanted. Precious little of that to be found here though."

"Wait a minute," I said, cutting him off. "Let's keep this real, all right? He's probably dead out in the woods. We've seen no sign of him since last night. The bullet probably lodged in something and the pressure kept him from bleeding out right away."

He shook his head. “No, Eric, you did him no real harm. It has been a long time, but I see things have not changed over there.”

“Over where?” I asked.

“They sent him for her,” he added, pointing to Jessica. She curled into my side further, and I put my arm around her protectively. “He is no mere wolf, but a hunter. They use them as assassins and trackers. They can find the stealthiest of prey. His task is to bring her back to them. And if he succeeds….”

“Who are they? Who is he?” I demanded.

“They are like us, yet different,” he answered. “Another world, Eric, like this one but so very different.”

I held up my hand. “Another world? Aliens? Come on, this is ridiculous. You’re scaring my daughter and probably just as crazy as your buddy Johann! I want you out of here,” I growled.

“Eric. Stop being childish!” he snapped at me. “Because you’ve been told they are fairy tales does not make them so. Where do fairy tales come from?” he asked rhetorically. I opened my mouth but he never let me say anything. “They came from us, that’s where! We created them and shared them throughout the ages, making people afraid of the unknown. Scaring children and keeping them afraid of the dark. Afraid of looking into things that are too dangerous.

“This other world is not here, in this solar system. There are no spaceships that I know of. They are from another dimension, parallel to our own. Very similar, yet very different. We developed technology, they developed in other areas.”

“Other areas?” I asked, not sure if I was hooked and genuinely interested or just humoring him until I could call the police.

"Yes," he said. "Powers we would call magic, for example. Some of them possess it, though many do not. Those that do are very dangerous."

"What?" I blurted out, taking a serious step into the realm of calling him a crazy old man.

"The women. More than a few of them are witches. They are born with it, you see. Men must learn to harness it, and it is no simple task," he explained.

"Your buddy Johann said something like that," I warned him, growing angry at how silly the conversation had become.

"I understand everything you have been led to believe tells you I am wrong," he said to me, his eyes showing some compassion. "But all you have to do to know in your heart I am right is to look at the beautiful young lady beside you." In spite of myself, I found myself look down at her. She glanced up at me, smiling timidly. "Already she's breathtakingly beautiful," he said. "Imagine how she will be able to stop the hearts of men with a simple glance in a few more years. And that is only a glimpse of the power within her.

"Eric, it started with you and with Karen. Karen came from a long line of refugees from…from there," he said, stumbling a bit. "Over two thousand years ago the last came across a great bridge between worlds. That bridge was sundered and sealed forever, and those that had crossed were trapped in what we now call Ireland. Not strong enough to enforce their way of living, to survive they had to blend in and toss their beliefs aside. Over the generations they forgot their past and became much as the rest of us.

"They were tracked and watched though, warders throughout the ages kept eyes upon them to ensure they did not remember. Once, hundreds of years past, there was an uprising. A girl was born with the spark of magic in her eye. My predecessors did not know the truth of it and we all suffered as she was used to open a small portal. There was considerable strife before that portal was closed, including the means of ensuring that none of the invaders survived."

"What was that?" I asked, eyes narrowing suspiciously.

He sighed and looked away, moisture gathering in his eyes as he said, "The bubonic plague."

I barked out a laugh that made Jessica jump a little beside me. "You claim your ancestors started the black plague?"

He shook his head quickly. "No, never that!" he protested. "The invaders started it and they used it to cover their movements. We defeated them and drove them back, but the plague remained. With so many dying it was simple to accuse others of being infected and have them added to the burning piles. That or to dispose of them secretly and arrange to have the body tossed on a cart." I relaxed a little, but still found the tale to be quite far–fetched. "Eric, I see you do not believe me yet. Tell me, what magic has Jessica done?"

I looked at her again and shook my head. "No magic," I said, denying him. "She's just good at music and dance and art. Turns out she's got a green thumb too."

I sensed her shift and I looked down at her. She was holding Percy up, who looked around nervously as all attention was drawn to him.

"He was dead last night," she whispered. Percy squeaked as though agreeing with what she said. "I took him with me and I was praying and hoping for my daddy while that wolf attacked. Before I knew it, I felt him moving and saw that he was alive again."

Jerry's hands were holding the arms of the chair he sat in and his knuckles had gone white. Eyes nearly bulging, he was unable to speak for several seconds at her revelation. Finally, he looked at me and asked in a steely voice, "Who were your parents?"

I did a double take. My parents? I frowned. "My mother's name was Gwen Young. She passed a few years ago from cancer."

"And your father?"

I shrugged. "I don't know. He left before I was born, I was told. My mother still loved him though, didn't blame him for running off. She even made sure I had his last name, Baxter."

Jerry stood up and started to pace. He was muttering to himself while Jessica and I just looked at one another, confused.

"I don't understand. If any of this is true, and I'm not saying it is, why do they want Jess?" I asked him.

He turned on me and scowled. "Of course it's true!" he snapped. "Stop trying to pretend you haven't seen what you've seen and heard what you've heard." He took a breath and calmed down a little. "I'm sorry. Look, the life of a warder is not one that is chosen, it is thrust upon us and we take it up because we must."

"There are always choices," I insisted stubbornly. "My life is my own to live."

He smiled ruefully. "Yes, there are. You could choose not to protect her. You could have chosen to let Johann finish her. You could have chosen to let the wolf take her back with him." I scowled at him. "There are choices, but not ones you could make," he finished, making his point. "That's why you are a warder too, Eric. You are Jessica's warder."

I looked to my daughter and she looked at me. She smiled uncertainly, and I gave her a one armed hug. "Crazy or not, looks like you're stuck with me," I told her.

She smiled broader and hugged me back. Percy made his squirrel noises and hopped into her lap to lay on her thigh.

"They want her because if they take her back, they will have forced a bridge open. It takes a powerful sacrifice to close a portal between worlds– on both sides. Once someone with the gift comes through it will stay open and can be widened with the passing of each new gifted person.

"If this wolf came from there, isn't it open already then?" I asked, spotting a hole in his logic.

He shook his head though, denying me. "The gift is what it is called when a woman is born with it. Only possessing it naturally, not those who learn it."

"Okay, so how did this hunter get here?"

"He is only here for a short time. A month, or from setting of one moon to the rise of the next," he explained.

"One day?" I asked, confused.

He sighed. "New moon to new moon, twenty-eight days. His time is nearly up. He has been here over three weeks, watching and studying you, He will remain for three more days."

Jessica whimpered and my arm throbbed. I looked at it, surprised. It was bruised badly where I had jammed it into the wolf's mouth, but that was the worst of it. I tried to remember if the skin had been broken last night and found I could not.

"But how could it get here in the first place? How did it find us?" I said, returning to my original question. "If no gifted person has come through."

"Eric, you are so suspicious. You have every right, I suppose," he added. "They would need something here, some act of lasting power, to show the way to this world. There are special times of the year when they can bridge the distance, but it is a fleeting moment. Other times, when certain conditions are arranged just right a greater window may appear. Is there...wait! This garden. Can you take me to it? I must see it," he said, suddenly remembering our tale of the wolf.

"What about the wolf?" I asked.

"During the day he will be vulnerable, like any of us. Unless desperate, he will only hunt at night."

"All right then, let's go. It's not quite noon, we'll be back long before dark," I said, giving Jess a pat on the arm to get her moving.

She hopped up, cupping Percy in her hands as she did so. He was on her shoulder in no time and I wondered at how his sharp little claws must be digging into her skin through her shirt. She showed no sign of discomfort though, so I just shook my head and rose up to follow her. I holstered my pistol and went to the front door.

Jerry came after us, following closely and looking around like a tourist. He was appreciative of the beauty, I suspect, but also looking for any sign of threat, though he had no idea what to look for. I had plenty of idea, but aside from the continued absence of animals in the area, nothing seemed amiss. We crossed the new bridge and stood upon the edge of the hill looking at her garden in a few minutes.

Jerry stared at it, moisture gathering in his eyes again at the simple sight. He was not moved by the death and discord surrounding it, but rather the beauty of the garden itself. Yesterday I had seen fresh growth, but it had been far from my mind. Now I realized how much growth it had been, for today her plants stood still immature yet with nearly a quarter of their full potential already reached.

"'Fertile ground', she called it," I told him softly, as though sharing a private joke. Jessica smiled in spite of her own sadness at seeing the dead animals.

He turned to her and sank down in front of her to his knees. "Young lady, I'm a foolish old man," he told her. "It's my fault you had to grow up without a mother, and I can't tell you how sorry I am. I-"

I couldn't stop myself. In a moment Jerry flew through the air to land on the ground with a role and a slide. I followed, intent on tossing him a few dozen more times. Maybe even using him for some wolf bait.

"Daddy, stop!" Jessica screamed, running and grabbing my arm to try and pull me back.

I growled and wrenched my arm free of her grip, then continued on my way as Jerry was orienting himself and trying to get up. Jessica jumped in front of me then and turned to face me. Percy had ran up a tree to hide.

"Stop!" she demanded again, holding her arm out and looking at me with a brave face.

I stared down at her then looked beyond, at Jerry. I felt a fresh rush of anger that made me clench my fists. He had admitted responsibility for Karen's death. I wanted-

"Daddy, remember what you always tell me," she said, bringing my attention back to her. "You always tell me that everything will be all right."

Reminding me of the silly phrase I used to make her feel better did nothing to silence the thundering of my pulse in my ears or relieve the strain in my fingers and forearms from how tightly my fists were clenched. I had stopped believing it at some point, maybe last Fall or maybe last night. Sometimes everything was not all right. Sometimes you just had to learn to cope and move on, but it would never be all right again, at least not the way it once was or might have been.

She turned back to Jerry and offered her hand to him. Looking anxiously at me, he stood up and then looked at Jessica. She smiled at him and nodded. “I’m sorry you felt you had to do what you did. I would have liked having a mother, I think.”

I looked away, blinking back my own sudden emotions that had managed to overcome my rage. I closed my eyes for a long moment and took deep breaths even as Jerry silently let the tears fall from his face at his own shame.

“We can’t change it,” Jessica said to him. “but we can learn. I forgive you, and in time my dad will too.”

He dropped to his knees again in front of her, whispering something in that language that was not English again. Jessica stepped closer to him and wrapped her arms around him, giving him a hug. Then she stepped back and leaned into me. She looked up at me and smiled and I felt my anger dissolving. The ache and the hurt was still there, but it was hard to feel gloomy with sunshine such as her shining on me.

“What did you say?” I asked him.

“*Banríona*,” he said. “It’s Gaelic for Queen.”

“Queen?” Jessica and I asked at the same time.

He nodded. “Most of us came from there. Not directly, of course, our ancestors. We believe in living life as it is lived here, free and without the tyranny and evil that sweeps through the lands over there."

"Wait," I said, interrupting him as he paused to take a breath. "What is this other place you keep talking about. It's another world, I get that, even though it seems impossible. But what is it called?"

"We call it *Dorcha Talamh*, the Dark Earth," he said. "It is much like this one in size and climate, but the people–oh the people are so different. Violence and fear rule that world. They have laws and nations and such, but they are a façade created at the whim of whichever cruel Lord is in power at the time.

"They want to come here because they want more land, more people, more wealth, and more power. And now I know how they found us. This garden is signaling to them. I barely possess any talent; there are few on this world that have learned any of the skills necessary to work the art. Still, I can tell that this garden is a beacon in the darkness. A lighthouse, if you will, lighting the way across the dark void between dimensions."

"So we need to destroy it?" Jessica asked sadly.

He sighed. "Yes-or find a way to hide it," he added. "It will not change that the hunter is here, nor that he has days remaining. But it will stop any more from finding us after he leaves."

Jerry started down the hill towards the garden. I watched him for a moment, then, my hand on Jessica's shoulder, we started after him. He paused at the edge of the savaged ground around it and took a breath to center himself. I heard him mutter something in that weird language again, Gaelic, I guessed from what he had said earlier, and then he stopped forward again to cross it.

There was a sharp crack as without warning the high warden's body was tossed through the air away from the garden. It sounded like a cross between thunder and an ancient oak tree snapping under the weight of snow and ice. I instinctively crouched down, shielding Jessica from the movement and noise, but aside from that I am ashamed to say I was just as stunned and uncertain as she was.

No further violence followed, though a faint smell of ozone and sulfur reached us. I looked around, seeing where Jerry lay near the edge of the clearing, and stood up slowly. Seeing nothing coming, I urged Jessica toward him, though she needed little encouragement. In fact, she beat me to the older man by several seconds.

"Daddy, he's hurt," Jessica whispered, kneeling down next to him to see what she could do to help.

Jerry was more than hurt, he was hurt very badly. It was not pretty. I wanted to pull her away and shield her from knowing what had happened, but it was too late. I dropped down beside him too, knowing there was no way to help him. He stared up at the sky, gasping for breath. His legs and stomach were a mess; it looked like...well, it looked messy.

His eyes settled on Jessica and he smiled in spite of the agony I expected he was in. Tears ran from his eyes and he whispered something to her, then he turned to me and grabbed my hand with his. The skin on his hand felt hot and raw, and a glance showed me it was red and blistered.

"Warden," he whispered.

I nodded and felt my own eyes filling with tears. I turned to Jessica and saw her reaching for him, hoping she could do to Jerry what she had down to Percy. I reached for her to pull her away and to me, but she fought me off and insisted. I had no choice but to let her, even though it broke my heart to see her fail. Jerry was gone, his body was so badly damaged even a team of the best surgeons in the world could never have hoped to fix him.

Finally I was able to pull her away. I held her while she sobbed in my arms. Looking around while she cried, I saw Percy standing on a rock, acting most definitely not like I would have expected a squirrel to act. He sniffed but stayed quiet, then finally, when Jess quieted herself and detached herself from me he scurried over to her. She looked down at him and then reached down to pick him up and, for lack of a better word, cuddle him to her.

I closed Jerry's eyes and turned to stare at the garden. It had looked a thing of beauty and, in truth, it still did. Now, though, it seemed a deadly beauty. Wordlessly, I put my arm around Jess again and guided her back to our house. We had a lot of things to do and think about, but right then neither one of us knew how to deal with any of it.

Chapter 7

Back at our house we stopped short. The door was open. I looked around suspiciously and felt as if there were a crushing hand on my chest when I saw the flat tires on my truck and Jerry's car. Every one of them had been slashed, and slashed with something that guaranteed a tire repair was impossible. I turned to look around, wondering how it had happened in the short time left and saw my barn. My breath caught in my throat as a sliver of hope surged through me.

We lived in an area that was known for harsh weather, and that required off road vehicles at those times. I pulled Jessica along with me to my our barn and saw both of our four wheelers sitting on their rims as well. Our two snowmobile were undamaged, but given the lack of snow, they might as well have been.

"Daddy, what are we going to do?" Jessica asked me. I squeezed her hand and knew I had to come up with a plan. The fear in her voice alone was enough to spur me into action, even if the thought of our very survival being at stake was not enough.

I reached for my pocket and realized even as I did so that my phone was not on me. I had never picked it up from where it was sitting in the house, on the bar. I scowled in spite of myself. "My phone is inside, wait here and I'll go get it then we can call the police."

She clung to my hand. "Daddy!" She hissed, scared at the thought of me leaving her. "Don't go! It's in there, I just know it!"

I expected she was right, but had no counter-argument. "Jess, we can't go anywhere without a vehicle. I'm not going to put you in danger."

"What if it's a trap?" she asked, her eyes narrowing. "What if we're supposed to think it's in there, but really it's waiting for us to separate? Daddy please, just stay with me," she begged.

I looked around, anxious to keep her from seeing the conflict and indecision in my eyes. I nodded finally, and we settled down to wait in the corner of the garage. At least I still had my gun, even if it was as useless as Jerry had claimed.

The better part of a half hour passed. The Spring chill started to seep into our bones. I felt Jessica staring up at me and finally I glanced down at her and smiled encouragingly. "Just like sitting in a deer blind," I whispered.

She shook her head, disagreeing with me. "Yeah," she said sarcastically, "only difference is that we're the ones being hunted."

My smile faded at her dark humor. To keep both our thoughts from turning too dark I decided I needed to bring up a different subject. The only thing that came to my mind was hardly a ray of sunshine though. "What did Jerry say to you back there?"

She stiffened a little next to me, then she swallowed loudly enough for me to hear it. "He said the garden was warded against anyone that meant it harm," she said.

"Warded?" I asked her, confused.

She nodded and whispered, "Yeah, I think it means it was protected. All the dead animals and the way the ground was ripped up around it. Must have been some magic spell the wolf put on it to keep the portal open."

"The wolf cast a magic spell that killed Jerry when he tried to go and destroy the garden?" First magic, then a wolf. Why not a wolf using magic?

She shrugged but stayed silent. I gave her a one armed hug letting her know that as crazy as things were, I was in it with her.

Time passed. I glanced at my watch and sighed. My stomach suddenly clenched at the realization of what I was going to do, but it had to be done and nobody was going to do it for me. “Come on,” I told her. “Let’s go find that phone. Otherwise we’ll end up stuck out here at night and we’re not dressed for it.”

There were other reasons I did not want to be outside at night, and she must have guessed them because she shivered and nodded. We climbed to our feet and cautiously made our way across the driveway and up to the house. Peering through windows we saw nothing amiss at first. Then, finally, I saw my phone. It was on the floor instead of the bar. It was smashed as well, the battery laying near it and the flipped up ear piece twisted at an angle.

Jessica’s breath caught in her throat, she had seen it too. “What now?”

I said nothing, but I pulled her after me as I approached the door. We entered very carefully and found nothing waiting for us. Never separated by more than a few feet, we searched the house from root cellar to loft and found no sign of intrusion except for my phone and the open door.

“I’m scared,” she whispered, hugging herself against me. I felt a strange movement and saw Percy stick his head out of one of the pockets on the front of her jacket. I could tell he was afraid too, not of us, but of the wolf. I tried to remember when he had come back from the tree he had climbed, but nothing came to me. I filed it away as unimportant, compared to the dangers we were facing.

I found myself sniffing, and for some reason I had an impression that someone unfamiliar had been there, which we already knew, but they were gone now. I looked at Jessica and Percy, then shrugged and went to push the door shut.

"Daddy, what are we going to do?"

"We secure the house," I told her. "It's not made out of straw-that wolf won't be blowing it down."

She stared at me with a look that practically screamed at me for daring to try and make a joke out of our situation. I smiled weakly and began to move about, looking for ways to bar doors and windows. I had plenty of spare lumber in my garage, but the thought of going back outside made my normally sea-worthy legs tremble. Taking Jessica seemed an even greater risk.

"Dad, he's not here right now," she told me.

I nodded. For some reason I could not explain, I shared her hunch. I thought for a long moment then went to the kitchen and started going through the drawers.

"What are you looking for?" she asked me.

"Silver," I mumbled, picking up silverware and tossing it aside as I saw stainless steel etched into it instead.

"You believe him?" she asked, her voice soft.

I pushed the drawer shut and went to her, kneeling so that I was looking directly into her eyes. "Sweety, I may be a stubborn old man, but there's no way of explaining how he went flying through the air and got hurt the way he did."

"I told you, he said it was a ward-"

I held up a finger to her lips, which normally made her cheeks burn red and her eyes turn even redder with anger. This time, thankfully, she accepted it, which I appreciated since having her scream at me right now would not have been in our best interests.

I smiled. “I know, I’m giving him the benefit of the doubt because I can’t find a good reason to doubt him anymore. You can bet I’m going to try to find more reasons to doubt, but until I do I’ll accept anything and everything.”

“Even what he said about me?” she whispered.

I hugged her. It was longer than we should have spent, but it felt like the right thing to do. Finally, when we pulled apart, I said, “The part about you being special, absolutely. You’re going to go on to do some amazing things, young lady, and I plan to be around to watch you do them as long as possible.”

She smiled and her eyes watered. We hugged again, briefly, then I stood up. “All right Princess, you ready to do this?”

She nodded, her hand slipping once more into mine. I heard Percy squeak and could only shake my head at how uncanny his behavior was. It was like he understood us too.

We went back out, heading to my garage. I cast my eyes about looking for a sign, but saw nothing unexpected. I found myself smelling and tasting the air as well, though it made no sense to me. There was nothing troubling about it, other than the fact that I was doing it.

Two trips later we had carried in several boards, screws, a hammer and nails, and my cordless screwdriver. I had a spare battery that was charged, but little hope that it would make it through the afternoon.

As we were about to board ourselves up Jessica called to me and got my attention. "Daddy, what about Jerry?"

"Jerry's dead, honey," I reminded her gently.

She gave me a look that implied a considerable doubt of my intelligence. "I know that. We can't just leave him out there."

"Jess, if we had a phone that worked, we could call the police. If we had a truck, I'd be happy to haul him to it and take him in to town, but we don't," I told her. "It bothers me," I said. "I mean, what will the police think when we do get in touch with them? Why did we wait, they'll wonder. And our story–not much chance of them buying that."

She nodded, frowning as she thought about it. "What do we do?"

"I'm not sure," I admitted. I shrugged and smiled at her. "It will work out, might take some hard work, sweat, and tears, but it'll be okay."

"You always say that," she reminded me. She was beginning to sound like a broken record and I imagined that was exactly what she thought about me.

I grinned, deciding to push it a little farther. "And so far, have I ever been wrong?"

She stuck her tongue out at me and I laughed. Somehow, in spite of everything, we shared a precious moment. Perhaps we clung to it even more desperately than usual. Given the events and the looming evening, I could only wonder when we might have a chance for the next one.

We boarded up the windows and the front door. My back door consisted of a sliding patio door on a small deck that overlooked the small stream a dozen feet below and a few hundred feet in the distance. I put a few boards across that one too, ignoring the screws and nails that went into the woodwork. I only had to remind myself once that the house could be replaced or repaired; Jessica could not.

We finished securing everything and then I went back and double checked it all, adding extra reinforcement where necessary. Finally, realizing I was doing neither of us any good, I went to my gun safe and took out the other firearms I owned. One was a bolt action Remington seven millimeter hunting rifle, the other a Browning twelve gauge semi-automatic shotgun. I had a bow as well, but I doubted it would be of much use given how fast that wolf was and the lack of silver broad heads.

"You remember what Jerry said, don't you?" Jessica asked me as I finished loading the weapons.

I grunted. I remembered, and it seemed he had been right. Still, just giving up was not my style. "Yeah, I know, but it's all we've got."

"No silver?" she asked.

I shook my head, the silverware was all stainless steel. I had a few silver dollar coins stashed away in some drawer or other, but those did not seem likely weapons.

"He said something enchanted would work too," she said softly.

My first instinct was to say something witty and sarcastic but I curbed my impulse and took a deep breath. "Honey, I guess maybe, now, I can accept such a thing is possible. But there's nothing like that here. I mean, we don't even know how that's possible or how to use something like that. It's hard for me to even believe in the thought of it."

She nodded, but then she climbed off the chair she was on and went to my gun safe. I watched her, curious, as she reached in and pulled out my hunting knife. It was an eight inch long Buck Knife that always held a great edge.

"What are you doing?" I asked her, curious and a little concerned.

"I don't know," she admitted. "But it can't be any worse than what you're doing."

I scowled at her, which prompted that same tongue being stuck out at me. "You're not going to be that close to that thing," I told her.

She nodded and agreed with me. "I hope not!"

"So hand it over, I'll hold on to it, just in case."

"Just a minute," she said, drawing it out of the sheath and staring at it. She nodded and smiled. "Okay, give me some time, okay? I want to try something."

"You…what?" I asked her, wondering what she was going on about.

"Dad, please!"

I looked heavenward and sighed. "All right, just be careful. We've got enough on our plates right now, I don't need to worry about you cutting a finger off."

There was that look again that one day she would use to silently promise her future husband a night spent on the couch, at best. I would have laughed at any other time, but I was too afraid she might not have a chance to meet the lucky guy who could be her future husband.

She went back to her bedroom and spent several minutes in there. I was getting nervous and ready to follow her, even though I heard her rustling around opening drawers and such. She came back out, an armful of stuff in her hands, and set it on the table along with the knife.

"You're going to paint some pictures on it?" I asked her, incredulous.

She shrugged. "I see something in it, I can't explain it. I'm going to do what I did with the garden," she explained. "I saw something, a picture, I guess, in the ground and I just worked at it until it looked like what I saw. Kind of like carving or sculpting, I guess."

"And how's that going to help us?"

"Well, look what the garden did," she said.

I grimaced. That garden seemed to be a major source of trouble in our lives right now. It had even killed Jerry and, by providing some weird means of travel for this hunter that stalked us, it might be the thing that got us killed as well.

"I'll try to make this work for us, not against us," she added, her mind following the same thoughts mine had.

"Good plan," I muttered, then found myself moving to look out the windows. The sun was dipping behind the trees and the moon was already up, though it was only a small sliver in the sky. Three more days and we'd be free. Assuming we could figure out how to destroy the garden, that was. Otherwise they, whoever they were, would send the wolf back. Him or something worse.

"We'll head out tomorrow when the sun comes up," I told her. "Walk into town and stay at a hotel, or with Jack or something. We'll have to be safe there, there's no way a wolf can come into Marquette."

"Dad!" she admonished me, looking up from her work. "I really need to concentrate, this is harder than I thought."

I nodded and muttered an apology, then went back to pacing around and staring out the boarded up windows, looking for any sign of our attacker. Before long I found myself at the table though, staring down at the knife as she worked on it.

Before my eyes the image took shape. A few lines became an outline, and then details began to emerge. Before I knew it I was staring at the beautiful picture she was painting onto the blade. Both sides of it too, a mirror image. A wolf was leaping on it, mouth open and teeth ready to snap. It was two dimensional but with the opposite side of the wolf on the other side of the blade, it seemed to jump out of the steel.

A howl split the silence. The wolf was close, just outside the front door by my reckoning. We both started a little in surprise, so wrapped up in the painting were we. I looked around and realized I had been so caught up in what she was doing that the sun had set entirely. Her brush was in mid-air at the time, so no damage was done to the painting.

I turned, shotgun in hand, and moved to the front door. I stopped, something overwhelming me and making me angry. I shook it off, wondering what was the matter, and found I had a hard time moving closer to the front door. I peered through the cracks between boards but saw nothing. What I smelled, on the other hand, was unmistakable.

"Daddy, what is it?" she whispered.

"He just peed on the front door," I told her, "marking his territory, I guess."

"Gross," she said, then bent her head back to the knife and tried to hurry and finish it.

I stalked around, hearing occasional signs of snuffling and once even the scraping of something against a window, probably a paw. I snarled triumphantly. "looks like we did a good job," I told her quietly. "He can't find a way in."

Shattering glass and a solid thump against the boards covering the window in my office tested my statement. The boards held, and a growling noise showed the frustration of our attacker. I rushed to the doorway and stared at it from there. I saw movement through the cracks between boards, but then nothing as it moved on.

"Here daddy," she said, surprising me that she was so close to me.

I looked down and saw her holding the knife up to me, hilt first. "Be careful, it needs to finish drying."

I nodded and took it from her, marveling again briefly at the beauty and life of the painted wolf. "You sure this is going to work?"

She shrugged. "I felt something when I was painting it," she said. "I don't know how to explain it…just…well, something."

I nodded and hugged her with one arm. "That will have to do then," I said, and I moved back to the table and set it down carefully on it. "Let it dry more," I told her. "Just my luck I'd get wet paint on my hand and it would make my grip slippery."

She nodded, then cringed when another crash sounded from the patio doors. Somehow he had managed to climb onto my deck. The lumber held, but we heard considerably more growling before it moved off.

"Should we hide in the cellar?" she whispered to me.

I shook my head, though I had thought of that myself. "There's no way out but through here," I whispered back. "Always make sure you can get away."

She nodded, accepting my apparent sage advice. It made sense to me, though I do not remember getting it from anywhere or anyone in particular. Perhaps from hunting and fishing I had learned it. Trapped, you stood little chance except to fight, having an escape route meant you had options. I was no coward, but fighting against something that seemed unbeatable made for long odds.

A few more scrapes and thuds shook our nerves, but then it went strangely quiet. Minutes passed and suddenly I could tell we were alone. I glanced at my watch, it was only half past nine.

"Daddy?" Jessica whimpered.

"Shhh, we're alone now," I comforted her. "Not safe, but for the moment there's no danger."

"What are we going to do?"

"Let's see if we can't get a little rest," I told her, though I knew that sleep would be difficult to find. "We need to be at full strength tomorrow."

She nodded, though she looked as doubtful as I felt about the prospect of falling asleep. I had no intentions of it, actually, but I hoped she could have a chance to rest at least. I moved to the couch and she curled beside me, resting her head in my lap. I rubbed her back soothingly while I listened and watched, wondering how long our respite would last.

* * * *

I woke up to a silence so deafening it seemed as though a falling drop of water would be heard around the world. The stress and anxiety had apparently taken their toll on both of us; Jessica slept in my lap with a blanket crocheted by her grandmother pulled over her. It was chilly; the fire had died out because we had been so caught up in defending ourselves that I'd forgotten to stoke it. A glance at my watch showed only a few hours had passed. A few hours that, in Northern Michigan at night, could induce hypothermia.

I looked around, watching the windows. I knew he was back. I could just tell, somehow, that he was there. I paused, realizing I was once more sniffing the air, and wondered again what it was about him that I could somehow smell. I saw nothing, but I felt a sudden sharp intake of breath from my daughter and glanced down to see her eyes wide open and staring up at me.

"The wolf's back," she whispered.

I nodded. I wondered if she could smell him too.

"Do you know where?" she asked softly, her eyes traveling to the spots she could see.

I shook my head. "How do you know it's back?"

"I just do. I can feel him, he's ugly, daddy. Ugly and mean."

I nodded. Mean was right: my leg and arm, the arm especially, were still sore from my encounter with him the night before. "You don't, um, smell him, do you?" I asked her a little nervously.

She looked at me oddly. "Smell him?" she asked. I nodded, and she shook her head. "No, I just can tell when he's close. It's like he just makes the air feel wrong. Why? Can you smell him or something?" she asked.

I nodded. "Musky, powerful. He's an alpha male, used to making others do what he wants them to."

She raised her eyebrows. "That's weird. Kind of gross too," she said.

"Very weird," I seconded. "Never been able to smell things like that before. And don't ask me about your shampoo."

She twisted around on the couch and sat up, looking at me with narrowed eyes. She leaned closer, invading my personal space as she stared at me.

"What are you doing?" I asked her finally, ready to retreat from her intrusive gaze.

"There's something different about you," she said suspiciously. "I'm not sure what…just different. Not like you're dangerous or anything. You just seem more…I don't know, more natural?" She frowned, not finding the words for what she wanted to say. "Like you're more a part of all this or something," she said, gesturing around herself to indicate the near wilderness we lived in.

"Sweety, I'm the same person I've always been. Don't worry, nothing is changing."

She shook her head. "Oh, you're the same, but there's something different in you now, too. I bet you got it when the wolf hurt you."

Living in a nightmare as we were, her words made my mind go to some pretty fantastical things. I wondered just what she could possibly mean, or worse, what I could be turning into. I nearly laughed when I realized where my thoughts were headed. It sounded crazy! Things like the creatures in my mind, creatures out of horror movies, did not exist.

Then again, neither did magical gardens that opened tunnels to other worlds and sent unarmed men flying a dozen feet through the air to a gruesome end.

"Stay here," I mumbled, getting to my feet and reaching for the shotgun that leaned against the couch. She whimpered but stayed.

I let slip a word from my mouth that I would have taken back, if I could. Jessica paid it no mind though, but instead she joined me near the front door. There, sitting against the side of my truck, were two people. The sky was clear and the moon nearly set, but the stars gave us light enough to see they were tied up, both gagged and bound. One was a boy and the other a girl, in the late teens I guessed. They were so terrified I could almost smell their fear.

Then I realized that was exactly what I could smell, their fear.

"Oh my gosh!" Jessica hissed, her hand coming to her mouth. "Daddy, we've got to help them!"

"How does a wolf tie up two kids and drag them up here?" I asked her, suspicious and torn.

"Maybe a man bit him sometime," she said.

"Jess, be serious," I admonished her.

"I am!" she snapped. "Look, a wolf bit you and you've got something going on with you. You don't want to admit it, but I can tell, okay? So maybe somehow that wolf can act like a human at times. At least enough to tie a knot."

I wanted to dismiss what she said as even a possibility, but we were already living in a world that had not existed a few days ago.

"Fine, maybe, but what about them?" I asked, gesturing with my head in their direction.

"We have to help them," she said.

"It's a trap," I told her. "An obvious one."

She nodded. "I know, but it's not fair! What makes our life worth more than theirs?"

"Fair is a concept dreamed up by some lazy guy who wanted the same benefits that someone who worked hard had earned," I said, wishing it was that simple and hoping that saying the words aloud would make it so. It didn't.

I turned and looked out at them. Probably college kids or high school sweethearts out camping or hiking. I looked closer, but it was too dark to make out good details. I glanced back at Jess then moved just enough so she could not see me clearly. I sniffed, pulling in the air and letting myself study it.

The only new scent I pulled in took me a minute to recognize. When I did I gasped. It was blood. The girl's blood. She had been hurt.

I growled, not wolfishly, just out of anger. "All right," I told Jess, and I went back to get the knife from the table. The paint was dry, so dry, in fact, that it looked like it had become a part of the blade itself. I sheathed it and quickly unclasped my belt so I could wear it. Thus armed, I picked up the shotgun from where I had let it lean against the table and moved back to the door.

"Jess, screwdriver," I said, pointing to where the cordless screwdriver was on the bar nearby. She grabbed it and came over, trying to unscrew the boards as quietly as possible.

In the still night it sounded horribly loud. I expected the wolf to be waiting outside, perhaps around the corner of the house. Neither of the kids seemed focused on anything, they were looking all over the place, and occasionally at the girl's leg. In the shadows I thought I could just barely make out a dark spot on her pants. It seemed she had been hurt in the leg; that must be the blood I smelled.

Finally the door was free. I turned and pulled her into a fierce hug. "You stay right here, you got it?"

She nodded.

"It will be okay. I'll get out there, grab the kids, and get them back in no time. You shut that door behind me and wedge a chair against it, okay?"

She nodded again and threw her arms around me. "Thank you daddy!"

"Just be sure to open it up when we're back," I reminded her.

She nodded and moved to grab a chair from the table to wedge against it. I peered outside, looking and sniffing, but I could not find my adversary. He was out there, somewhere, but I did not know where. I pulled open the door and started out, shotgun held ready and the safety off. I moved cautiously, trying to find him. The kids saw me immediately, and started squirming and making muted noises behind the ropes in their mouths. They drew my attention even though I knew I should be ignoring them.

I reached them without incident. I motioned for them to stay quiet, then took a final look around to see more of the same menacing darkness I had already seen. I knelt down and set my shotgun on the ground beside me. The knife came out and I grabbed the rope. It felt odd to me, made of a very fine fiber which was neither hemp nor nylon. It was warm to the touch too, although not uncomfortably so. What really stunned me was when I put my knife to it how the rope actually shivered in my hand and acted as though it was trying to get away from the blade.

I sawed faster, cutting through it and making the entire rope go slack all of a sudden. The knots released on their own and it slithered to the ground almost like a dead snake might. The two I had just rescued looked at me in amazement, but there was terror and tears in their eyes as well.

"Back to the house," I hissed at them. "Can you walk?"

The boy nodded, the girl shook her head. "Here," I said, handing the boy my shotgun. "Safety's off," I warned him. He took it and held it like he knew how to use it; I was relieved.

The girl was over my shoulder then. I picked her up and turned back towards the house. Just in time, I heard glass breaking and then another crash, accompanied by the sounds of wood breaking, this time from inside the house. I nearly dropped the girl, but held her tight instead and ran towards the house. We hit the door and bounced off of it. The girl rolled away, yelping in pain. I was back on my feet and hammering the door again, moving it slowly. I heard Jessica scream once for me from inside, then heard the sounds of something crashing against my cast iron stove. Her next scream was cut off abruptly. I could smell him and, I realized, I could smell her. Not her shampoo, something else…her sweat maybe. I hammered against the door again and again, moving it half an inch at a time.

I heard wood being broken and tossed aside then nothing else from inside. I had the door open enough I finally squeezed my head and one arm through it. Instead of yanking the chair out of the way I stared at the shattered skylight and the broken coffee table. Likewise, the patio door had been broken through, the boards easily shattered from the inside apparently. The final explanation of sounds was a lamp that was broken and laying near the stove from where I presumed Jess had thrown it at him. I did not stop to wonder the details, instead I tore myself away from the door and took off at a dead sprint around the house. The teenager cried out from where she lay, begging me to wait, and the boy started to follow me then stopped, unwilling to leave her behind.

I leapt over the bridge, reaching for the pistol and finding it not there. I had taken it out when we sat on the couch to rest–I did not want her to be uncomfortable. The knife then, that was all I had on me. Just as well I figured, since it was the only weapon I had that might actually do something. The guns seemed to be useless since the wolf was uninjured either by me or the fall from my roof.

The leaves were only buds on the tree at that time of year. Because of that I could see further even in the gloomy shadows of pre-dawn. He was running ahead of me with Jessica caught up in his mouth. She was trying to shield her face from sticks and the ground and trying to punch out at him at the same time. He had her shirt in his jaws, holding her tight and preventing her from slipping out of it. I yelled, thinking to slow him down, but that only made him speed up.

Panting now, I topped the hill and saw them stopping at the border of the garden. The wolf's sides were heaving with each deep breath, and that made me feel a little better. I did not slow, I kept running. He and Jessica both watched me come. I saw her cheeks were streaked with tears. What amazed me most was that the carcasses of the animals around the garden were gone. A few tufts of fur remained here and there, but now all that remained was the rent earth and Jerry's body. His body had been dragged into the border surrounding the garden, however.

"Daddy!" she screamed, then squealed as he shook her with his powerful neck muscles.

"I'm coming!" I yelled, though it came out strained due to my lack of breath.

The wolf looked at me, then he looked behind himself, to the West and the brightening skyline. He took a step towards the garden and I, still a few dozen feet away, knew I was running out of time. I had seen what happened to Jerry when he tried to cross, yet I knew the wolf would not be affected by it because of what Jessica had said. Jessica cried out again and reached desperately for something. The wolf jerked her around again, disorienting her, and dragged her with him.

"Face me you coward!" I bellowed, closing over the uneven ground at breakneck speed. "I beat you once! I don't have a gun this time, or are you only strong enough to abuse a little girl?"

I was frantic. Anything could have flown out of my mouth, so desperate was I. I would have done anything right then, made any deal, happily traded my life for hers. My legs, lungs, or heart could give out, still I would run after her.

Imagine my surprise when the wolf turned to behold me again. It growled and jerked its powerful neck, sending my daughter through the air and into the border of the garden. She rolled and looked up, surprised and confused. She stared around, as though she was lost and confused. I cried out for her, and she looked in my direction, but acted as though she could not see me. He turned to face me, bearing his teeth and snarling. I laughed, then saw Jessica turn around, as though she heard something else. She took a step beyond the boundary and into the garden and disappeared from view.

She hadn't fallen, nor was she hidden behind the ridiculously tall plants that grew there. She simply vanished!.One minute she was there, then she was gone, as though she had never existed. I stumbled to a halt, mouth open. The wolf looked behind him at the garden and then looked back at me. His snarl looked like an evil grin.

I shouted something, I don't even know what, and I was running again. The wolf ran at me as well and we met in mid air. My teeth were bared as ferociously as the wolf's and there was surely no higher thought process then the instinctive animal need to destroy my rival in my brain.

The fight between us felt like it took forever but it may have been over in an instant. We fell to the ground and rolled around, him snapping at me and gouging with his legs. I punched and drove my knife into him. I felt him shudder and heard yelps as my knife sliced into him. I felt sadistic glee that Jessica had been right, she had given me a tool that could hurt him.

Finally I collapsed, exhausted and unable to move. I bled from dozens of places, both tears in my flesh from his claws and holes from his teeth. I had changed my clothes while we fortified our house, but now they looked worse than ever. Tattered scraps remained, stained with my blood and with that of the wolf. The wolf shuddered and breathed no more; my knife, slick with his blood, stuck in his side.

I lay there, gasping for breath and feeling pain in places I did not know I had. With every passing moment I tried to regain some strength, but as the numbness of adrenaline wore off I just felt more and more pain. My heart, hammering in my ears, was the only thing that assured me I was still alive. I rolled, finally, and looked towards the garden. I grabbed my knife, pulling it from the wolf, and distantly noticed that the painting Jessica had put on it remained as fresh as when she had first put it there.

Knife tucked in my hand, I tried to rise. Pains in my belly and legs refused me, causing me to lay there gasping. I was hurt, and it was bad. I needed help, medical help. I wondered if I was going to die there in the middle of the forest.

The thought made me growl in denial. If I died, no one would help Jessica. I reached forward and started to pull myself. I felt another tearing pain in my abdomen as I reached, but I ignored it and stretched further. The blackness danced at the edges of my vision and then, before I could fight it back, it claimed me.

* * * *

I woke up, which was a great start. Groaning, I swatted at whatever was irritating my face. The noise I heard made me open my eyes and look at the source. A small furry creature that, after a moment of focusing my fuzzy eyes, I realized was Percy.

That brought everything back to me, including the fight and the impossible pain my body had been in. I tried to get up and found my breath stolen from me for a moment. I still hurt. It was not as bad, but it was there. I forced myself, gritting my teeth in the process, into a sitting position and I looked at myself. I looked a mess.

My shirt and pants were shredded and brown with dried blood. As nervous as it made me, I pulled up the tattered remains of my t-shirt and very nearly blacked out again. Dried blood covered my wounds, but the wounds were not as mortal as I had expected them to be. Removing my blood-caked shirt had reopened some of them but the red tears they wept were not as bad as they should have been. Staring at them I saw that some of my injuries resembled my leg from the first run in with the wolf: a healed but fresh angry red scar. It was impossible. Even if I had slept for a day or two I would not have recovered this much.

A glance at my watch and told me that I had been unconscious for only ten hours. It was nearly four in the afternoon. There was no way those wounds could have mended in less than half a day! Last time, Jessica had used her...well, whatever it was she had used to heal me. This time there had been no Jessica. Just me, unconscious. I wondered if maybe that first time it had not been her either.

I gasped. Was it a horrible mistake? Was Jessica not the one who had the magic? Maybe all along it had been me and she had been taken by mistake?

I looked at the hunting knife laying on the ground where I had dropped it when I passed out. My eyes were pulled to the painting on the blade that was a part of the blade now. Jessica had done that, not me. She was the one. I felt a knot in my neck loosen in relief. I did not want to think what would have happened to her if whoever had taken her had found out she was not who he was after. Especially a person willing to kill so mercilessly.

"And you," I said, looking to the squirrel who was sniffing my side. I shook my head and in doing so, saw something that stopped me in my tracks.

I turned, groaning as I forced myself to my feet. My tortured body balked, but obeyed me. I stared down at my opponent. There, on the ground, lay a man. He was naked and showed signs of great injuries over his body from my knife. His hair, both on his head and chest, was dark but streaked with white, much like the coat of fur on the wolf had been.

"Impossible," I muttered, wondering if I would wake up from the fog that gripped my mind.

An angry squirrel chirping saved me from escaping into the realm of make-believe. He was sitting on the hilt of my hunting knife. I nodded and reached down, taking the knife after he hopped off of it and putting it back in the sheath at my hip. Then I held out my hand for the squirrel. Percy sniffed it, then hopped up on to it and let me put him on my shoulder.

"All right Percy, if she could go in there, then maybe so can we," I said, turning to face the garden.

“Let’s do this,” I told the squirrel. I stepped forward, then stepped again, crossing over the border of death around the garden. We passed unmolested. The protective spell that had killed Jerry had no qualms about us, it seemed. Then again, we did not wish the garden any harm. That would come later, after I had gotten her back.

Suddenly I found myself surrounded by a complete and total blackness. I wondered if, perhaps, I was wrong. Maybe the ward had just killed me? My step faltered and suddenly I understood why Jessica had not been able to see me. For some reason it was impossible to see out. Percy chattered in my ear, and for a brief moment I found myself wishing I could understand him. I took another step, careful to move straight forward. Three steps later we emerged from the darkness and into something altogether unexpected.

Chapter 8

"That's not Bodrik," said one of the men I saw standing in the clearing before me.

There were four of them, all dressed in a fashion I would have expected from someone in King Arthur's court. They wore layers of leather armor studded with bits of metal. Similar quality boots and gloves—gauntlets—I guess, and leather hats with a metal ring about them. Two carried crossbows and the other two had swords. I felt like I had stepped straight into a medieval movie scene.

"Aye, get the Mundling!"

The two with swords rushed me, but left their weapons sheathed. My hand flew to my knife and I snarled at them as I crouched low. I figured they were trained in hand to hand combat given the swords and such. I knew I was at a disadvantage because when it came to hand to hand combat, unless it was a large fish, I was out of my depth. Percy leapt off from my shoulder to the ground and ran for cover.

One tried to tackle me, but I dodged to the side. He still managed to hit me with a glancing blow, and my body ached all the more for it, but I stayed on my feet. The second man, surprised, tried to reach forward and grab me. My knife whipped across, cutting through the leather on his sleeve and making him yelp in pain. He clutched at his wound and fell back. I was not complaining about their choice to not use their swords; my knife would have been little defense against them.

"Loose your bolts!" he yelled to the archers. "He's too much trouble to capture."

I heard the sound of crossbows firing, but I was already ducking and running. They missed, though one came so close I felt the air shiver as a shaft passed by me and I could smell the wood of the shaft. I was in the woods before they could reload, ducking and dodging through the trees and underbrush.

I ran blindly at first, then I realized that my body knew where I was going. I recognized landmarks, not trees or plants, but the lay of the land. It was my land, more or less. I changed course, heading off, I hoped, deeper into the woods, away from where civilization was in my world.

I stopped running after a while, my lungs heaving and my body aching. I had left my land behind, but I had no idea where I was now. Jess and I had hiked across plenty of land, but we stayed clear of anything posted private. There were no signs on this world; nothing to stop me from exploring as I wished.

I checked the forest around me as I walked, peering through the trees to make sure I was not being followed. I saw that I had upset the ground behind me, leaving a trail that was clear to follow. Northern Michigan was littered with rocks I could use to hide my tracks, but my scent would be on them still. What I needed was a stream to be sure I could throw off any pursuit.

I smirked at my thoughts. Before being attacked by a wolf, I would never have thought to worry about being tracked by scent. My own sense of smell was heightened, in fact, which pushed my thoughts further. I could smell the wetness rising from the ground, the mold in the fallen tree trunks, and the fresh growth that spring brought. It was the same smells I had known before but they seemed fresher here. It was like things were more pronounced, more alive. More real.

I looked at my watch and saw that I had been here, on the Dark Earth, for nearly half an hour. With one last glance around to get my bearings, I headed in what was North back on Earth. I could only hope it was the same here. There was a stream I could use to hide my passage, then from there I had no idea where I was going to go. My only real thoughts involved heading back to the gate and seeing if I could find people to follow. I presumed Jessica would have been taken to whoever was in charge over here, and I had no idea what or where that would be.

Splashing through the stream was cold and unpleasant. Even more, I was worried about the quickly approaching night. I could expect to see frost tonight and with wet shoes and pants, I might be in trouble. I had neither matches or a lighter, no way of lighting a fire. I decided high ground might be my only hope, so after I finally emerged from the stream I made my way to the East.

The hike was the same as I remembered, and also much more difficult. The lack of trails was a complication, but it was the absence of daylight as the sun set which really made my climb onerous. I crested the peak of Hogsback around just after nine, nearly a full hour after the sun had set in the Western sky. Above the trees the slight wind chilled me further, reminding me that I should not have pushed myself so hard that I started to sweat.

I looked up to a familiar sky. The constellations were the same, yet somehow they seemed brighter and closer. I looked away, already thinking of the used camping spots that would have been present if I had been on my world. Most of them would have been made by college kids out for a night of partying-my experience in my own world was that they would have left behind something with which I could start a fire. Seeing the unmarred natural beauty of the land in this world, however, I frowned and hugged myself in an attempt to stay warm.

"Well, if cavemen and Indians could do it," I muttered to myself, deciding on a course of action. I headed for a flat spot next to a broken off chunk of rock that served as a wind break. I gathered up some sticks and a few small pieces of rock.

I spent the next half an hour trying to start a fire. Beating rock against rock earned me nothing but smashed fingers. Trying rock against the steel of my pocket knife was no better, just more dangerous. My hunting knife I kept at my side, safe from any thoughts of trying anything stupid. It was the only tried and true tool I had at that point, I was not going to risk it.

When the rocks failed I moved on to rubbing wooden sticks together. I got them warm, and it warmed me trying to do it, but the energy I expended made it a bad idea. That and they never came close to being warm enough to even smolder. I tossed them aside, disgusted, and tucked my arms into my sides. I ended up curling into a fetal position, hoping I would not end up with hypothermia before the night was over. Even after I finally drifted off, shivering, I still slept fitfully, trying desperately to find whatever warmth I could.

The morning found me stiff and cold to the bone. I could move everything, though, so that was a start. Somehow, in spite of the miserable conditions, I found my body recovered even more from yesterday's fights. I stretched myself out, finding minimal soreness, and found a perch to sit on while the sun worked its way over the Eastern horizon.

Watching the sun rise over Lake Superior never failed to steal my breath. This was no exception. Quite the contrary, this time around it was more poignant than ever. It lacked the sight of fishing trawlers heading out, smoke from factories in Marquette, and the distant noise of cars heading up county road 550 to the North. It was pure and natural in a way that made me hate my ancestors for ruining it on my world.

I let my eyes, squinting in the morning sun, drift towards where Marquette would be in my world. I saw another city, smaller and far more primitive, but a city nonetheless. Distant huts so small I could not make them out form one another dotted the countryside. They stood before something that distance could not distort, something I had never expected I would see. It was an honest-to-god castle. I rose and stared at it, my mouth open as I saw something that threatened to knock me from my feet with the sheer proof of its existence.

Once and for all I knew without a doubt that this was not my world.

--*-*

Before leaving the mountain-top I studied more of the land around me. Big Bay, the small town far to the North in my world, was too far to be seen given the lay of the land. In many other places I could see smoke rising from chimneys. Often the forest hid the houses from view, but in other cases I was surprised to see tracts of land cleared away for farming. That amazed me most, since the short growing season this far North usually prevented any sizeable yield on crops. On my world it was rare to see a backyard garden, let alone a field filled with corn or wheat.

I had made my way down, stopping at a stream and drinking my fill from it. On this world I reasoned the pollution would be practically nonexistent, making the groundwater safe. It tasted cool and clean, so I had no reason to doubt. I saw a brook trout at one point and realized I was staring at it hungrily. My stomach grumbled, unsatisfied with the water, and I could feel the saliva in my mouth.

I backed away, shaking my head in surprise. Sushi had never been my thing. There were plenty of ways I could catch some fish, from making a snare out of some vines or grasses to finding a stick to lash my knife to and use as a spear. The problem was, I still could not make a fire. Disgruntled, I moved on. I figured I could find something to eat easily enough at one of the houses I had seen. Already I could smell the faint traces of smoke on the wind, telling me where to find civilization. In a few cases the more savory scents of cooking food trailed with them.

I took to jogging through the forest, though it was really more of a lope. As I went, I caught other scents as well, things that nearly made me stop and wonder what was happening to me. I smelled animals, from squirrels and possums to deer, coyote, and even a black bear at one point. I had no idea how I could smell the animals, let alone know instinctively what they were. On a deep level it freaked me out. Fortunately, my body's hunger drove me on and made me not dwell too deeply on the strangeness of it.

In less than an hour of crossing the wilderness, I found my first cabin. Hand hewn from logs, there was a fire burning inside that promised so many things. It made me homesick: my own house back on my world was made of logs as well. Modern technology and building techniques made mine far more hospitable, but at this point a cave and a bearskin rug would have been a palace.

I could smell people, too. Three of them. A women and two young children. Their voices carried through the shuttered windows, and the things I heard surprised me. I had feared I might not understand them. After all, I was on a different world. Similar to my own, but for all I knew that was only on the surface. Like the soldiers I had first encountered, and managed to escape from, they spoke English. Perhaps it was not quite as modern and filled with slang as the one I was used to, but it was easily passable. Their accent was not like I was accustomed to either. By that I mean I was expecting the traditional Yooper accent, which boasted a strong mix of Scandinavian in it. Theirs was free of any such traces. Instead they sounded like anyone from the mid-West might expect to sound.

Recovering from that shock was easy. It was the way that the mother spoke to her children that really left me stunned. On my world her behavior would have been considered abusive in a heartbeat. She followed it up at one point by beating the girl, calling her useless and a disgrace to their family and insisting she should have at least had the decency to be gifted if she was going to saddle them with the uselessness of being a girl in the first place. She capped it off by telling her daughter that she could barely wait until the poor girl was thirteen and could be sold off to some foolish man as a wife. I sat back, hidden behind some trees, and felt stunned. I could not imagine treating a child like that.

The boy came out with a bucket to fetch water from a well at one point. The girl followed soon after, hanging laundry. The boy picked up where their mother had left off berating his sister when she let one of the clothes drag briefly on the ground. He went in, his bucket full, and I found myself being drawn to the little girl.

"Psst," I called to her, moving behind a shed. "Honey, what's your name?"

Okay, so back on my world such an approach would at least be creepy. At worst, I would be accused of having a bag of candy and some pretty sinister intentions. It made me wonder whether the people on my world really were so much better behaved after all.

She looked at me, jumping a little in shock. She saw me and squinted. "Avery," she said uncertainly. "You wear strange clothes."

She looked to be about six years old, I figured. Far too young to be verbally or physically abused like she was.

"Avery, I came from a place very far away and I'm lost. Can you tell me where I am?" I asked her, speaking softly and smiling.

I could see her thinking. There was something in her expression that concerned me. More than just the reluctance of a child talking to a stranger, she seemed to be calculating something in her mind.

"Are you a spy?" she asked.

"What? No!" I said, surprised. "I'm looking for somebody, for a little girl in fact. She's my daughter and she was taken from me."

"Taken from you?" she repeated. She stepped closer to me. The clothes in her basket were forgotten for the moment.

"Yes, by a bad man. I think she was taken to that castle, but I don't know. Can you tell me who lives there?"

She giggled. "That's Lord Baxter's castle. He rules the land. My father says he's rotten to the core, just like everyone else, but at least he knows where he stands with him. Father also is mad because Lord Baxter is smart and he makes it hard for him to lie about what he makes so he doesn't get taxed as much," she confided with a smug look over her shoulder at the cabin, as though she was getting even with her family in some sneaky way.

"What did you say his name was?" I asked, stunned by what I had heard. Was I really going crazy? Was I really on another world, or was I strapped into a chair in a hospital somewhere having delusions.

"Lord Baxter," she said.

"But that's…that's my name," I mumbled, confused.

"You're Lord Baxter?" she asked, eyes going wide. She turned, nervously, and looked towards her house.

"No!" I said quickly. "I mean, my last name is Baxter. I'm Eric Baxter. My daughter is Jessica Baxter, she's the one that was kidnapped."

"Only Lord Baxter has two names," she said uncertainly, starting to back away.

"Wait!" I hissed, reaching for her. I calmed myself and called to her again. "Wait, Avery, please. This Lord Baxter, does he have many guards? Or a pet wolf?"

Her eyes widened. She stepped back. "His huntsman, Bodrik," she said. "He's a changeling."

Bodrik was the name the guards had said when I first came through. "What's a changeling?"

She stopped, surprised. "You don't know what a changeling is?" I shook my head, though I was fighting against a nagging feeling in the back of my head. The wolf I had fought and the man I had discovered when I awoke. What Jerry had told us and what Jess had insisted upon. It all made sense and I was having a hard time denying it. "They're demons," she said, speaking softly. "Able to shift from man to animal. Lord Baxter uses Bodrik to hunt down criminals and outlaws."

"Well you don't need to worry about Bodrik anymore," I told her.

"Are you an outlaw?" Her eyes narrowed.

"Not where I come from, anyhow," I muttered.

"Did you kill Bodrik?"

Half of Jessica's age and she was asking about whether I killed a man? I wondered how early children were forced to grow up here. Apparently by age thirteen. I stopped, staring at Avery in horror. Jessica was thirteen. Was some forced marriage planned for her? Perhaps this Lord Baxter wanted her for that.

"Avery, I have to find my daughter. Do you know anything about the castle?"

"You did, didn't you?" she asked, cracking a sly smile. "You killed Lord Baxter's huntsman."

She turned and ran for her house. I reached for her, foolishly since she was so far away, calling out for her to stop. She ignored me or perhaps did not hear me. Either way, she was gone. I heard her shout for her mother, telling her about me. She was yelled at, at first, but by the time her mother came out to check I was gone.

I moved away and around the house. To save Avery from further punishment I left a scrap off my shirt and obvious footprints in the dirt. She might have turned from me, but I could not blame her. She might have seemed just as crafty as her mother sounded, but given the way she had been brought up, perhaps that was not so surprising. And even so, I could not be a party to a child being bullied.

I slipped away from the cabin, heading in the direction of the castle. I was still ravenously hungry but I began to have doubts as to just how easy it was going to be to find help. If everyone here was as twisted as the family I had just seen, I was in trouble. Worse, Jessica was in even more trouble.

I stopped in mid stride, nearly crashing into a tree. I remembered what Avery had said about Bodrik. She had called him a changeling, called him a demon that changed from a man to an animal. In his case, a wolf. I shuddered. It was impossible. Sure, I had seen his body laying where I had killed the wolf, but it could not be real, could it? It was a myth. A legend told to scare children. I stopped, my thoughts going blank as I refused to remember what Jerry had said. Finally, reluctantly, I consciously let the memory come to me. I let him tell me again how the legends had to come from somewhere.

I slid down the tree and sat on the ground, putting my head in my hands. Even now I could smell the loam beneath me and the fresh water from a nearby stream that I could not yet see. I could smell the mark on a tree left by a stag claiming his territory. Changeling was not the word used on my world for what Bodrik was. He was called something that was impossible. Something that could not exist. He was called a werewolf.

My stomach growled, driving me to my feet with a sudden pang. I had no idea what was happening to me, but my body knew it needed food. I moved off, sniffing the air for another cabin. Another place where I might be able to find some food. Somehow I knew that there was one not so far away. I wanted to understand how I knew it, but that would have to wait until I could focus on something other than how hungry I was.

I ran towards the smell, feeling the thrill of the forest air as it passed me. I reveled in the thud of my feet on the soft ground and the feeling of power in my legs and arms as I bounced from rock to ground and pushed away from trees. I found myself thinking about food-first things I was familiar with and then, when I caught a scent of something, thinking even of the meat of wild animals. It was terrifying and invigorating, all at the same time.

Breathing heavily, though still far more easily than I had any right to, I emerged from the woods and into the clearing of another cabin. This one was empty, I knew. The door was shut and the shutters were closed. I realized I was growling as I walked a circle around it, testing the door and shutters. I wanted in; I could smell food inside.

Finally, lacking a better way, I used some firewood stacked beside the cabin as a battering ram. It took several attempts, but finally I broke open the latch on the door. Tossing the log on the ground, I stepped in and looked around. It truly was something out of the dark ages. No running water, no modern amenities at all. That included no refrigerator and no electricity. Even the bed was just a pallet filled with pine boughs and straw under a coarse sheet.

I followed my nose, finding a basket with some terribly stale and dried out bread in it. It was less than half a loaf, but I did not care. I tore into it, eating savagely. I found a clay jug filled with a foul smelling liquid, but I reasoned it was probably some sort of mead or ale. It had been a while since I had drunk any alcohol-nearly thirteen years, in fact. I had never been an alcoholic, I just needed a clear head and the ability to function. Now I did not care. I drank deeply to wash down the bread.

I found other things as well, salted meat that was equally unpalatable, yet I ate it like it was prime rib. Some roots and even a potato, which I ate raw. It was crunchy but sweet and juicy. I had never known a potato taste so good, especially uncooked. I guessed that I would never taste another like it, since it had to be due to how ravenously hungry I was.

Finished and finally sated, I looked around again and felt some remorse. I had just broken into someone's house and stolen from them. I felt terrible, and then even worse when I realized I had nothing to offer as repayment. The scraps of paper in my pocket used as money on my world were useless here. I had come across a few roughly minted and pressed copper coins while I went through the cupboards looking for food. They were the size of a quarter on my world, but thicker and not nearly as uniform in shape and consistency.

With nothing else to do, I tried to tidy up the damage I had done and then left. I thought, briefly, of stealing some clothing as well, but I found very little to offer and it seemed to fit a man smaller than me. I wanted at least to write some note of thanks and apology, but the savages of this world had no paper and pencil. I reasoned they probably could not read or write either, and filled with disgust for this world, I moved on.

My next stop had to be the castle. I had to steal my daughter back before she became too deeply entangled in whatever nefarious purpose this Lord Baxter had in mind for her.

Chapter 9

On my way to the Dark Earth equivalent of Marquette, I managed to find a change of clothing, snatched from of the clothes lines of some random house in the wilds. Unfamiliar with the crude clothing, I wore it as best I could. A pair of pants to replace my jeans were held up with a tied leather cord. The shirt was loose fitting and made of deer hide, which I knew made for a stretchy leather at best. Wearing peasant's garb, I hid my own under a rock at the edge of a river. Then I made my way into the city, Lord Baxter's realm.

I wandered amongst the shops and houses, trying not to wrinkle my nose at the smells that assaulted me. I had begun to think my new senses were wondrous, now I doubted the wisdom of that. The things I smelled were the reeking chemicals used for tanning hides, the stench of meat left too long in the sun, and the glory of a lack of public sewers and sanitation.

I wandered about in a daze with my senses overwhelrmed. I had not noticed it before, but now I realized I was hearing differently as well. At first, surrounded by all the sounds of the city, it was disorienting and maddening. After stumbling about a while, though, I learned to make sense of it, and by tilting my head I soon found I could focus in on specific noises. This included conversations that were not meant for others to hear, which was how I learned a great many important things.

The common folk of the area were mostly concerned with simple ideas. Food and work first, then gossip second. The city guards that wandered about were more useful to me, for they hinted at rumors of the Lord's missing huntsman, or of how plans were underway to use the gate to Mundania now that it had been opened.

Mundania, it seemed, was what they called my world. It had originally been a stroke of dark humor about the lack of magic practiced there, but by now it it was simply what it was called. As much as it annoyed me to have my home referred to so facetiously, I realized that by calling this world the Dark Earth, I was doing the same thing.

It seemed everyone wanted to talk about the bridge to my world, and the talk led to dreams of conquest and plunder. Even the most average of citizens seemed to think there was untouched land for the taking on my world and that gold ran in the streams. People also showed more than a passing interest about the rumors of a man coming through the gate. A man who had escaped the guards through treachery and stealth and was even now being sought. Rumor had it he was dangerous; speculation was that he had killed Bodrik, the Lord's changeling.

I grinned in spite of myself when I heard these things. It was good to be considered dangerous, though I would have rather nobody knew about me; it would have given me a better chance of finding and rescuing Jessica

My stomach grumbled again as the day wore on. I checked my watch, which I had taken to carrying higher up my arm under the sleeve of my stolen shirt. It was nearly four in the afternoon. I had lost most of the day already and I felt as though I had accomplished nothing. I glanced about, wondering how I would eat again.

In the past, especially when out on my fishing boat, I would go twenty four to thirty six hours without eating and not be bothered. Ever since I came here though that seemed impossible for me. I had never noticed hunger as powerful as this. I still refused to consider what it meant, but it was getting harder and harder to ignore the obvious implications.

I wandered into a shop that did not smell as bad as the rest of them did. Immediately it was obvious that I was in a smithy. Various tools could be found around the room: spades, plows, knives, horseshoes-even a few swords and crude pieces of armor behind a counter. I looked them over and saw a young boy, roughly Jessica's age, behind the counter.

He was eyeing me, waiting for me to approach him. I considered what I might ask when I heard noises in the background. I tilted my head, and quickly enough heard a conversation from the back of the shop. From the smell of smoke that came, I knew the smith's forge was back in that direction.

"How much did he pay you?" growled a voice.

"Master, I thought that-"

"No, you didn't," said the first voice, angry and resigned at the same time. "You know I have a charter from Lord Baxter. You saw an opportunity to make some coin. How much? I pay you, and that's more than any apprentice receives. More than you deserve, maybe."

"Master-"

"Enough!" barked the smith, his voice cracking a little with the strain. "Perhaps I should send you back to your father."

"Please Master, I thought this would give you more orders!"

"More than I have time to do. You're not as dumb as you pretend. Remember this, Jarid, I run a fair and honest shop. I'll not have an apprentice that ruins my reputation. I'll think on whether I keep you, but for now get out of my sight!"

I heard some muttering, then a door shutting. I found myself chuckling at the apprentice's behavior. The conversation gave me hope for if there was at least one person here that believed in fairness and honesty, then perhaps all was not lost. With my hopes buoyed for the first time since I had arrived, I nodded to the boy behind the counter and made my way out of the smithy and back onto the street. I was back to being hungry, alone, and poor.

I made my way down to the docks. My goal was to invade the castle and reclaim my daughter, but it had to wait. I could not ignore the gnawing hunger any longer. I figured the docks were my best bet. I was a fisherman, though from a different place with different technology. Regardless, the fish would be the same, and I would be able to understand Dark Earth fisherman better than anyone else on this forsaken world.

It took me three ships and one brush with nearly being skewered by a gaff before I found a captain who could use me. He eyed me suspiciously, but I was getting used to that. It seemed nobody held any measure of trust for anyone on this world. It was only after I offered to accept as payment a single fish that he agreed to let me help. Given how hungry I was, and that I hoped not to be on this world much longer, I felt certain I had the best of the deal. What I had not realized was how primitive their fishing was.

The hold of the ship was filled with bins. There was no simple or efficient means to move the fish from the bins to the docks. No cranes with nets or buckets and no wheeled buckets capable of making it down the stairs into the hold. It was a painful process that took me and the four deckhands, who sneered at me as little better than a beggar, nearly two hours to empty the hold. Throughout it I had to grit my teeth against the occasional hunger pangs that threatened to double me over.

Finally finished, I accepted as payment a single lake trout. He was shy of two feet long, but weighed at least four pounds. My mouth watered in spite of the fact that he had yet to be gutted or scaled, let alone cooked. I thanked the captain and hurried off, clutching the fish in my hand possessively.

I wandered along the shore until I found a rocky section that was uninhabited. I was not yet far enough North to reach the peninsula I would have called Presque Isle. I could see it clearly less than a mile North of me, and rising from the middle of it I could see a small fort with walls made of vertical wooden timbers, and a lighthouse. I wondered about it, briefly, but reasoned that the castle where Lord Baxter was said to hold court was my target.

Finding one of many flat rocks, I lay my soon-to-be dinner upon it and took my knife out. With skilled–if a bit shaky–hands, I scaled and cleaned the lake trout. I cast about, wondering again about cooking the meat. But before I knew it I had apparently given up. I was eating the flesh of the trout raw, and reveling in the strong flavor of it. I knew, in my mind, of the parasites that could be in it, but I did not care. It was only when I felt my teeth breaking rib bones that I realized I had to gain some control of myself. I had given in to a feeding frenzy.

Stepping away from the rock, I stared at the savaged fish and found myself breathing heavily. I licked my lips and wanted more, but I forced myself to remain calm, or at least try to. After several tense moments the urges passed and I found myself feeling sated. My belly grumbled, happy this time, and I wondered how I could so easily stomach the raw fish. I shook my head, knowing I should be disgusted with myself, but despite that knowledge, I still did not feel that way.

For the briefest of moments I wondered what other dietary changes I could expect. Would I be chasing deer through the woods and tearing out their throats with my own teeth? I growled and shook the thought away. If I was cursed to be a...well, cursed with whatever it was, I would deal with that later. For now, I accepted it gratefully because it offered me new strengths that I could use to my advantage. A curse at any other time, for now I hoped it would be the edge I needed to overcome the challenges I faced.

I turned away from the beach and headed back up. I caught an unfamiliar smell and, for a moment, hesitated. I looked about, wondering; then a fresh breeze from the lake blew it away and made me wonder if I had imagined it in the first place. A final suspicious glance and then I headed back into towards the town. Night, I expected, might be the best time for me to make my attempt on the castle. Already the sun was setting in the West. With it came the chill of the Northern evening, but I found myself less bothered by it now than I had been before, even so recently as yesterday.

I caught the hint of a scent again as the wind died down and I climbed over the rocky bank of the bay. There was something familiar to the smell, a mixture not just of the scent of the person himself, but of coal and steel mixed with it. It was someone that had worked in that smithy. My eyes narrowed and I had a hunch that I had blundered across the trail of the boy that had been cast out of the smithy earlier.

Before I knew it, I had dropped to the ground and was sniffing it. I looked around, making sure no one was nearby to see me, and sniffed harder until I picked up traces of the scent again. I looked up and saw footprints that led towards the small fort with the lighthouse. Sighing, I climbed to my feet and moved along the trail. There were other scents along the way, but none were the least bit familiar to me so I paid them no mind. The original scent grew stronger as the cart path of a road wound up onto the rocky land. What had been a hunch had solidified into certainty in my mind.

I was so caught up in tracking the scent that I almost stumbled upon the people. I had walked into a stand of trees that surrounded the path, but realizing theywere thinning out and about to end, I stopped. I stared ahead, seeing the great wooden doors to the fort only a few dozen feet from me. Standing outside the wooden wall, which was only a dozen feet high at the most, were a boy and a man. I listened to them carefully, picking up most of their hushed but strained conversation until I fell back away from them. I had heard enough.

Now I had a plan. It was a weak one, but it only required the help of one person. And now I had something to barter with. Once I was far enough away I broke into a jog and from there into a run. Just like in the woods, I felt my lungs expand and the wind rush through my hair. It felt glorious to be running through the woods. I leaned forward and put on some more speed, my boots feeling clumsy and heavy. I was tempted to take them off, and nearly stopped to do so before I realized what I was seriously contemplating.

I dropped back to a walk, my breathing easy considering the couple of miles I had just run. I looked at my boots and laughed. They were work boots, not designed for jogging. Taking them off, though, would be silly without running shoes or something else to put on. I laughed again and walked into town, ignoring the images in the back of my mind that suggested I go barefoot.

The smithy was closed, and a casual knock on the door earned me nothing. With a snarl I walked around the building, heading down the sort of dark alley that I would have normally steered clear of. Nothing threatened me, so I moved on to a small clearing behind the shop. I found a wooden fence around the backyard, and soon enough found a door that was locked from within. I looked around, frowning, and then reached up. The fence was only about eight feet tall.

I grabbed the top of the fence, and with a jump easily lifted myself up and over it. I landed lightly on the inside and looked around, my hand going to my knife just in case. I saw a shed and a well in the backyard, and nothing else aside from a door into the smithy. I moved up and reached for the latch, lifting it slowly and carefully.

Before it slipped free I heard a hissing noise beyond the door. I paused, wondering what it could have been. I heard some more strange noises, metal against wood, and wood against wood, though none of it sounded dangerous. I lowered the latch and moved quickly to the door in the fence. I unlatched it and opened it a little, giving myself an escape route if needed, then walked back to the smithy and knocked loudly on the door.

The noise inside the building stopped. I heard somebody muttering something, then the door opened and I was staring at the sharp and pointed end of a sword. My first instinct was to bat it aside. I did not know where that urge came from, but I managed to avoid giving in to it and instead slowly held my hands up.

"Are you the Master Smith?" I asked carefully as I looked beyond the weapon to the person wielding it.

The smith seemed a regular enough man. He had an average height and build, though he wore padded clothes that protected him from the heat. A cloth was likewise wrapped around his face, protecting his nose and mouth from the fumes and heat of the forge that was glowing behind him. His hair was wrapped in another rag that reminded me almost of the turbans worn by Muslims on my world, save that it was only wrapped to keep the hair and sweat out of his face. That and one strand of fabric looped low enough to cross over the smith's left eye, much like a patch.

I looked around. The strong stink of the burning coals and fuels disguised most of the smells, but I could still make out the scent of the smith. Working that closely to such heat, especially considering the constant hammering, I would have thought would make him quite an unpleasant person to spend time around. Expecting the worst, I could not explain the absence of the foul manly body odor I was expecting would overwhelm me.

"I am. Who're you?" the smith asked me, his one eye glaring accusingly at me. "And what're you doing in my backyard?"

"I think you're a rare sort of man," I said to him, stepping back as he threatened me with his sword. The cool air at my back already felt wonderful compared to the stifling heat in the forge. "I have some information for you."

"I locked that door," he said, pushing me back enough to see past me into his backyard. "You jimmy the lock?"

I shook my head. “Lifted the handle and opened it,” I explained, which was true, though I left out the fact that I had done so from inside. “My name is Eric,” I continued, not wanting to waste any more time. “I overheard your apprentice a little while ago talking with someone.”

He stopped, eye widening then narrowing again. “What do you want?”

“Want?”

“Yeah, you wouldn’t be here if you didn’t want something. Everybody does.” He spoke gruffly, and I began to think his voice sounded a little off.

I sniffed the air again; the hairs on the back of my neck were up. Something was wrong with the smith, something that I could not quite put my finger on, even though I knew it was staring me in the face.

“Well?” he snapped, his voice breaking a little as he raised it-much like it had earlier when he had yelled at his apprentice.

“You deliver your goods to Lord Baxter?” I asked him. He nodded. “I need to get in that castle,” I said. “That’s what I want. Let me take your next delivery there, tell me what I have to do, then I’ll do my thing and you’ll never have to worry about me again.”

“What are you going to do?”

I ground my teeth a little in frustration. Finally, with my own eyes narrowed I leveled with him. “There’s not many people around interested in giving a young person a chance. Nobody cares much, except about themselves.”

He nodded, not showing much interest in what I was saying. I sniffed and caught a hint of something though-curiosity, perhaps. I told myself to make sure I never offered to play poker with the smith, he seemed far too good at bluffing.

"Lord Baxter stole something very important from me. I want it back."

He looked at me and I could see his jaw working beneath the rag he wore as a mask. "What is it?"

"Does it really matter? I don't want to hurt anybody, I just want what is mine back, then I go and leave this place alone."

"What's this news you think I need to hear?" he asked.

"We have a deal?" I pushed. I had seen and heard too many bartering sessions on this world already to leave myself open. I figured I only had one shot, and I was not going to miss it.

He shrugged. "You're asking a lot and I don't know anything about you. I need to know whether what you've got is worth a damn."

I nodded. He had a point, as much as I did not like to admit it. "All right, but what stops you from walking away once I tell you?"

He shrugged again, but I could sense a smile under the mask. "You'll just have to trust me."

I did trust him. Even thought there was something wrong about him, I had an instinct that said he would not lie to me. I leaned in closer, sniffing again, and stuck out my hand as an excuse to get closer.

"We got no deal, stranger," he said, looking at my hand and then at me.

I smiled. "Maybe not, but I think you're right, I think I do have to trust you."

Hesitantly, he reached out with his right hand and clasped mine, shaking it gruffly. He squeezed hard too, even though my hands were bigger than his. He never bothered to take his gloves off either.

"I heard your boy talking to a man by the lighthouse," I said, smiling as I caught a fresh scent of something. It confused me for a moment, but then I put all the clues together and suddenly had my answer.

"He promised to make you short your order to Lord Baxter so that he'd be angry and cancel his contract with you," I said.

The smith cursed. "That explains a lot," he said at last. He looked at me. "How'd you find this out again?"

"I was walking near the docks and saw your apprentice sneaking down the path to the lighthouse. I was in here earlier; I was going to ask for a job so I might make some money to buy a meal. I followed him, since I heard you had some problems with him when I was in here."

He nodded slowly. "Didn't think I was that loud," he said.

"I have really good hearing." He grunted. "Do we have a deal?" I asked again.

He looked at me and lowered his sword. "Lord Baxter finds out I helped you do whatever it is you plan on doing, I'm done for."

"He'll never know," I pledged.

"You daft? He's got witches that can ferret out a lie. And nobody's ever escaped his huntsman, so you won't be able to get away if he sicks him on you." I chuckled. "What's so funny about that?" he asked, irritated at my disregard for the serious nature of the conversation.

"His huntsman? Bodrik?"

"Yeah, that's him."

"He's dead."

The smith looked at me suspiciously. "He's been missing, I've heard, but he's a changeling. He can't be killed, they say. What makes you sure he's dead?"

I tapped the knife at my side meaningfully and said, "I killed him."

"You…you're daft!" he hissed. "Whether it's true or not, I don't want you near me. Get out of my shop and never come back! I see you again, I call the guards!"

The sword was back, pointing at my throat and uncomfortably close. This time I did reach up to it slowly and push it away. The smith was strong-years of hammering metal into shape will do that to a person-but I still managed to easily maneuver it away from me.

"He will never know, and you will help me," I said. I could hear him drawing in a deep breath, preparing to call the guards. "Or your secret will be revealed," I said quickly before the cry could be issued. Then, calmly, I finished my threat. "After all, who in this town will do business with a woman?"

Chapter 10

The smith's breath hissed through open lips. The cry of alarm died as quickly as the urge to give it had been created. "What?" the smith asked in a tone that was carefully neutral.

I could smell her fear. The sudden panic that threatened to overwhelm her nearly did the same to me. Something stirred within me, something that I did not recognize. It urged me to pounce on her, verbally if not physically.

"How do you keep your apprentices from finding out?" I asked her, curious and pressing my advantage.

"What are you talking about?" she said, her voice raising and cracking a little as she tried to pressure me into believing myself mistaken.

"I'm talking about that," I said, referring to her cracking voice. "I'm talking about the fact that you're not a man, and you're pretending to be one in order to do business with other men!"

My voice was serious but I kept it quiet so others would not hear. She stared at me angrily, then I saw her expression change. Within seconds I smelled the change in her mood as well. She was still afraid, but there was more to it, there was a calmness that surprised me. She looked past me nervously, then backed up and motioned me in. I followed, shutting the door behind me.

"Who are you?" she asked, reaching up to drop the rag over her mouth. Her lips were dried out from the heat. There was nothing over feminine about her jaw or lips, yet at the same time it did not look masculine either. She continued to pass, visually, for a man.

"My name is Eric," I told her. "I'm not from around here. I could care less that you are a woman."

She nodded and took the other rag off of her head and her eye. Her left eyelid was scarred. It looked like it had been burned and healed poorly, in fact. She kept her lid closed but I knew the eye beneath would never see again. Her hair was short, clearly cut by herself, and did not lend any femininity to her face.

The overall picture, however, was too androgynous to be a man with enough testosterone to beat a hammer and anvil all day long. I might have suffered from sexism, but I had never once seen any sort of blacksmith that was not large, strong, and possessed of a large amount of body hair. And this was the first time I'd ever seen a woman in that profession. For her part, she did look broad shouldered and strong. Without good genetics giving me a strong frame I would have probably been afraid to meet her in a dark alley.

"Much better," I told her, smiling. "Please believe me, I don't care that you're a woman. In fact, I think it's great that you're doing this. This place needs shaking up, it makes my stomach sick to see people living like this." Her good eye narrowed disbelievingly. I stopped talking, realizing that while I spoke the truth, I was letting her know too much about me. "What's your name?"

"Krystan," she said.

I nodded. "It's not my business, but how did you come to be a smith here?"

"I helped my husband," she said, not hesitating to tell me. It seemed she was anxious to get her story off her chest, in fact. I was surprised, but I suppose after keeping a secret for a long time it only makes sense that she was happy to divulge it to the only person who had guessed. “He’d been a journeyman smith for two years and had saved up enough coin to start a small forge of his own. He went North, crossing where the Westlake and Eastlake meet and found a small town several days ride NorthWest of there. They needed a smith and he had the skills. He had no money and was not proven enough to earn an apprentice, but he did earn the right as a skilled man to a wife. I had turned thirteen a week prior and he bartered with my father for me. I learned the trade helping him, and to save costs he kept his operation small. That and he need not worry about any competition starting up in the small town either.” I nodded: it made sense, in a dark and pessimistic point of view. “He took ill with consumption and never recovered. I tended him until he coughed his last,” she said. She showed no signs of sadness at his loss, but given that she claimed he had purchased her from her father, I could understand her lack of emotion. “I had nowhere to go, so I kept to smithing. It worked for nearly two months, then I was found out. They burned out my eye as punishment and banished me.

“I came here, after two weeks of walking with everything I was allowed to take, plus some that they had no idea I had. Started up a smithy here and proved I knew what I was doing. There was some others in town, but I stayed out of their business and stuck with simple things. Shoes and plows for horses and the like. Tools for the working sort. Wasn’t long before I got more business, and then my first order for a sword. They liked it, and from there more and more came. One of the other smiths headed off, looking for new fools to buy the scrap metal he called good work.

"Been here seven years now, and you was the first to know I'm not what I said, but I stick to the back and let my boys handle the sales."

"I'm impressed," I said to her. "I mean, to live a lie that long. It's sad really, but I am impressed with your dedication."

She almost smiled, but nodded instead. "What are you really after?" she asked me.

I did not have to tell her. I had her in the palm of my hand, actually, but given everything she had told me, I found myself wanting to share as well. "My daughter," I said.

Her eye widened as she made the connection. "That's the witch Bodrik went after then?"

I nodded. "He took her, but I caught him before he could escape too. Then I came after her."

She gestured around. "See all these weapons and shields? Lord Baxter ordered them for his men to take with them."

I looked around and saw the many swords in open barrels that she had pointed to. Shields, wooden planks bound in round iron frames, leaned against the wall in the corner beside the barrels. I lost count after a dozen, and I was less than a third of the way through.

"How many?" I asked her, staring at them.

"He ordered sixty sets, sword and shield, from me. He wanted more but I told him I could only do so much."

"When?"

"Another five days the order is due," she said.

"Five days," I muttered. "You send these in five days?"

"Yes."

"Take me with you, it's a large load, you can use the help."

She sighed and looked troubled again. "If you are caught, I'll be held as a partner and killed.

"What's more, if you succeed, I'll be held as a partner and killed," she added. "Or do you plan to kill Lord Baxter too?"

I had not considered that. He was the source of all my problems. Even if Jess and I were to escape and somehow close the bridge, he would try again. I shook my head. "Killing's not the solution."

"You killed Bodrik," she pointed out.

I sighed. "That was self-defense. I had to come after Jess and he attacked me."

"But you don't think killing Lord Baxter would solve your problems?"

"It would," I admitted. "But it's not my way. Neither is kidnapping a child."

"She's only a child? How can she be a witch?" she asked, confused.

"She's thirteen, she's really been coming into these powers a lot recently," I said.

"Thirteen is the age of adulthood here," she said. "Most women realize their full powers, or full potential, when the change is upon them."

"The change?"

She gave me a look with her one eye that spoke volumes. "Men," she sighed. "When a girl becomes a woman?"

"Oh!" I said, blushing and clearing my throat in hopes of hiding my obvious discomfort. "That, yes, well…okay. Wait," I said, realizing what she had said. "Thirteen is the age of consent?" She nodded. I whistled. "That's…well, it's eighteen where I come from."

It was her turn to be surprised. "Most women have three or more children by then."

I held up my hand. She spoke of things that were uncomfortable, at best, to me. Terrifying if I spent any time associating them with my daughter. "I don't want to make your life difficult," I said, changing the subject quickly. "Can you tell me how I might get into the castle safely?"

"Walk in," she said, not understanding.

"I don't know enough to come up with a convincing story," I tried to explain. She just looked at me blankly. "You mean I can just walk in the gates without being harassed?" I asked, confused.

"Yeah, as long as you aren't waving a sword or screaming, the guards won't look twice at you."

My world had metal detectors and armed guards requiring security passes to go anywhere. I'd figured this place would be even worse, given the nature of suspicion and mistrust in every person I had encountered here.

"Do you know where he is keeping her?" I pushed, hoping to get lucky.

"Somewhere in the castle, I'm sure. A servant or guard could tell you, but then they'd run and tell someone you asked."

I frowned. "All right…well, thanks." I had no more to say and I did not know what else to do. I turned to leave but then a thought occurred to me. "Can I trust you?" I asked, nervous.

She laughed, smiling in a way that made her pretty in spite of her butchered hair and years of attempting to look like a man. "I expect I got the better end of the deal, Eric, why would I push for more?"

I nodded appreciatively. "This world would be better if more people were like you," I told her.

She blushed a little but brushed it aside with a sharp laugh. "Not likely," she said, "but I expect if your world has people like you in it, it is a better place."

"It is a good place," I said. I glanced around, realizing it was time for me to leave. "Good luck," I told her, then stepped out the back door and pulled it shut behind me. I was through the door in the fence quickly, then heading up the alley and away from her shop, hopefully never to see it again.

I made my way through the darkening streets towards the castle. When I made it there a few minutes later I saw plenty of traffic, but everyone was coming out, no one was headed in. I took a deep breath to calm my nerves and walked towards the open gates.

"Ho, you there!"

My teeth ground against each other and my fists clenched. Had Krystan lied to me? Had she tricked me, removing me as a threat to her business? I was tempted to run but I knew I would lose my only chance if I did. I thought back and realized that the smith had not lied to me intentionally, her fear had been real. It seemed could already tell when somebody was lying just by how they smelled and acted.

I kept walking but the guard approached me even as I passed under the stones that connected the wall overhead.

"I said hold up," he growled at me.

I stopped, noting that the other guards, one more at the gate and a few on the towers on either side of it, were looking at me.

"The castle's closed and I don't recognize you, what's your business?" he demanded.

Of course, the castle was closed. It made sense, public servants had office hours, why wouldn't Lord Baxter? From what I had seen, he was hardly a public servant. He preferred the public serve him.

"I'll come back tomorrow," I said, turning away and kicking myself mentally for drawing attention.

His hand clamped onto my shoulder, pulling me back. "What's your business, friend?"

I turned back, forcing a fake smile even though my heart was hammering in my chest. I felt fear at being found out and at having no good excuse, yet that was washed away with the rush of fury that spread through me and warmed my limbs at the realization that he was touching me.

"I was going to ask Lord Baxter about a fishing charter," I lied. My eyes stared at his hand then looked into his face. I was nearly snarling at him; my lip trembled.

He stared at me for a long minute, suspicious but put off by the look in my eyes. I could smell a bit of fear in him; I had a hunch he was uncertain of what to do.

"Fishing charter?" he asked. A glance to the other guard confirmed that he did not want to pursue the matter, but he had gotten himself into it now. He was worried about what the others might say if he backed down from a commoner.

"Aye, I just worked for Captain Raynor, I've plans to get my own boat. I know where the best fish are, I wanted to speak with Lord Baxter about a charter to supply his kitchen." I knew where the fish were in my world, here, I could only guess they might be in the same place. It did not matter really, since I had no intention of doing any real fishing here. I told the lie with ease, staring into the guard's eyes and challenging him to call my bluff.

He grunted. "Come back tomorrow, the court opens at highsun."

I nodded. "Thanks," I grumbled, and walked away.

As the anger from adrenaline faded, anxiety and fear from what I had narrowly avoided filled the void. I rubbed my hands together to disguise the shaking in my hands and found I had no idea what to do or where to go. I could spend the night in the wilderness again, but doing so would hardly be my idea of a good time. I needed the time to think, though. I had to figure out how I was going to break into the castle during the day, find Jessica, and get away. And all of that without me knowing anything about the castle.

I walked long enough to find myself back at Krystan's smithy. I tried the front door again first, with the same success as before. I went to the back door, vaulting over the fence with ease. I listened and heard Krystan still hammering. I knocked on the door and heard her curse, then a moment later the door opened to reveal her standing there. She lowered the rag when she saw it was me and shook her head.

"Thought I was done with you," she said.

I shrugged. "Castle's closed for the night," I said. "I need a place to stay."

"Don't see how that's my problem," she said.

"I'm no stranger to hard work, show me what I can do to earn a spot on your floor for the night," I offered.

She looked me up and down appraisingly. Then, making a decision, she nodded and backed up, allowing me to enter. I followed, grateful, and listened and watched as she told me what to do and how to help. What followed was four hours of the most backbreaking work I had ever done. Shoveling coal, working the bellows, hauling water, and burning myself on hot steel as I ferried it about for her. I said nothing, aside from the occasional hiss or grunt as my fingers were burned. Nonetheless, by the end of the evening I felt myself at least five pounds lighter from the sweat that poured out of me. I had expected her to stink earlier, now I found I was the one that was in need of a good scrubbing.

"You're a good worker," she admitted as she banked the fires of the forge and drank a cup of water.

She handed the ladle to me and I gratefully dipped it into the bucket I had pulled from the well and drank deeply from it.

"You sweat like a pig though," she added, her eye crinkling with humor.

I chuckled. "I'm a fisherman, I'm used to hard work, but the heat nearly put me under a few times. My shirt's off to you for doing this everyday–you're a better man than I!"

She laughed in spite of herself. "I find that a lot."

"Pity, I expect you'd make an even finer woman," I added, taking another drink.

She blushed, though it was almost impossible to tell in the reddish glow from the fire. My sense of smell confirmed her embarrassment, but I did not push it.

"You've earned a spot on the floor, not in my bed," she said gruffly.

It was my turn to blush. I waved her off. "Clean you up and I don't doubt you're a pretty girl, but I'm not here for that."

"You prefer boys?" she asked, surprised.

"What? No!" I protested. "I have a daughter, remember? I just…her mother…"

She looked at me without expression and I realized that she might have actually been propositioning me. Seven years since her husband had died and she had been forced to live as a man. Seven years without any intimacy with another person. I could understand, though my own celibacy was self-imposed.

"Sorry, perhaps another time, in another place, I might have tried," I told her.

She shrugged and turned away. "Clean yourself with the well," she called out to me as she headed up some stairs.

It was an excellent suggestion, I headed into the yard and lowered then raised the bucket. I glanced at the door once self consciously, then took off my shirt and poured the bucket over my head. I washed up as best I could and, as refreshing as the cold water was in the night air, I quickly began to feel cold. I hurried back inside, trusting the heat from the forge would dry me off.

Waiting for me on one of the benches was nearly a quarter loaf of bread sitting beside a bowl filled with stew. Some clothes were folded up as well. I looked around but did not see Krystan anywhere. My stomach rumbled, having caught the scent of the stew. I spared no time in devouring it, easily ignoring how hot it was. When the bowl was dry and my stomach pleased, I checked out the clothing and found them to be a simple set of tunic and pants. Slightly more presentable than my stolen clothing. I changed quickly and then made myself a spot on the floor and used my old clothes as a pillow. In moments I was asleep, exhausted by the full meal and hard work of the day.

I woke up only a heartbeat before Krystan's hand touched my gently on the shoulder. She jerked, surprised, as my own hand grabbed her wrist. I let go immediately, realizing who she was, and looked around. It was dark in the room, only the ruddy glow of the banked coals in the forge gave off any light.

"It's morning," she whispered.

"Where I come from this is still night," I grumbled, rising to sit up and stretching my neck. "I'm sorry," I quickly added, realizing I was a guest in her house. "Thank you for letting me stay…and the food. And the clothes."

She smiled. "You earned them, I'm back on schedule thanks to your help."

I nodded and stood up. She had not donned her working outfit for the day and, though the light was poor, I saw that she was pretty. A muscular figure hidden only by her bedclothes, and no soot or ash on her face to disguise her femininity.

"You are a pretty woman," I said to her, a little embarrassed even as I said it.

She looked away quickly, but smiled. When she looked back she sighed, but thanked me. "It is good to hear, even if you feel you owe me."

I shook my head. "No, I mean it."

She shrugged. "It is no matter. Even if I were to dress in skirts with a face like this no man would call on me, at least not the type who's willing to stay more than a few minutes in my bed."

"What? Your eye?" I made a rude noise to show what I thought of it. "Any man worth the title would look past that."

She smiled sadly. "Your world must be wonderful, If such a thing is true there."

I chuckled. "Well, maybe not wonderful, but you'd find someone, I'm sure."

"Go," she said, standing up quickly. Her tone turned serious. "Find your daughter and take her far from here. Before anything happens to her."

I nodded and rose as well. "I will. My thanks, Krystan. I…"

She put her finger to my lips. “Go.”

I nodded and grabbed my knife, then put my boots on. I don’t know what I was going to say, but I suspect it was for the best that she stopped me. I had no intention of ever coming back once we were gone. And likewise, there was no chance of her following after us.

A pretty woman in spite of her scar? Yes, she was. She was kind and fair in a world filled with sharks as well, something that marked her as special. It was that kindness to me that I had a hard time so easily turning away from. I told myself I just hated to be indebted to someone, but there was more to it than that. I hated to feel that I had used someone, especially someone that seemed so genuine.

I finished strapping my knife to my side as I emerged from the alley beside her shop. The sun had yet to crest the Eastern sky, but I could see it beginning to lighten on the horizon. I had plenty of time to wait: noon, or highsun as they had called it, was at least five hours away.

I made my way down to the docks. It was what I was most familiar with, so I figured I would start my day there. I watched the sun rise and the ships load full of people and equipment. One at a time they pulled free of the docks, some with sails and others with oars. By the time they had all gone I guessed I had whiled away a couple of hours. The sun was still far from its highest point, but I was anxious to get my task underway. The longer I waited, the more my brain tried to wander into areas I was not ready for it to go to. Everything from wondering about myself and what was happening to me to the smith.

A line was forming at the gates by the time I got there. I was nowhere near the first, which I took as a relief. I did not want to draw any more attention to myself. I stood patiently and waited, mentally counting off at least a half an hour before I felt the hair on my neck rise again.

I glanced around, sniffing instinctively as I did so. The people near me in line seemed harmless enough, but something was amiss. Far off I heard faintly, "There, with the strange boots."

I glanced down. My boots were strange compared to everyone else. Made of quality materials on my world, there was nothing hand stitched or primitive about them. I frowned, realizing I should have changed them somewhere along the way. I wondered why Krystan had not said anything about them to me; surely she had seen me put them on this morning.

"Fisherman!" I heard a guard call out.

I looked at him and saw it was the same guard from last night. I glanced around, seeking escape routes. There were people behind me but I saw no sign of other guards nearby. If I wanted to, I could try and run for it.

"Step out of line, someone wants to talk to you," he said as he closed with me.

He was less than ten feet away and I knew running was no longer an option. People near me in line stepped away quietly, abandoning me to my fate. My hand itched to reach for my knife but I knew better than to give him a reason.

"He'll have to wait," I bluffed. "I'm waiting to talk to Lord Baxter."

"Nobody waits," he spat out. "Either you come on your own feet or we drag you."

My lip curled up and I growled before I realized it. There was something in me that wanted me to lash out at him. My fists clenched before I stopped them and forced myself to relax. I reminded myself that I had to play this right. Messing up would cost me my chance to save Jess.

I took a deep breath and forced myself to relax a little. "Who wants to talk to me?"

He barked a laugh, then answered me in a threatening voice. "The Lord's inquisitor. He always gets the answers he's after."

I knew he meant torture, and I knew that he would get whatever answer he wanted, no matter how long it took to beat it out of me. My eyes narrowed again and I looked around, taking my eyes off of him. That was a mistake. I sensed movement and tried to look back but not in time. He had grabbed my shirt and yanked me forward. My hands went to him, trying to push him away. I punched out and felt my fist slam into the steel on his helmet. It made my hand go numb.

I tore myself away though, somehow, and stumbled backwards while he shook his own head to clear it. "Stop him!" he screamed as I backed away from him.

I pulled my knife free, prepared to defend myself, and looked about for the best direction to run. I had no idea what to do; I only knew that getting away was my first and most important priority. Time suddenly stood still for me. I was moving in the same slow motion, but I heard something that sounded odd. I tried to identify it even as I looked for it.

It was the sound of air moving and wood hammering against wood. A muffled whistle of air and then steel against stone beside me, then the solid smack of steel into flesh. It reminded me of shooting a deer with my bow, only this time I was on the receiving end. I jerked around partially, a feathered wooden shaft suddenly appearing just under my clavicle on the right side of my chest. I felt the tip thud into my shoulder blade almost after the fact. In pain and off balance, I fell to the ground. That wrenched the crossbow bolt in my shoulder and made the barbed point grate against bone. I gasped, seeing colored spots in my vision, then felt no more as the guard cuffed me on the head with the hilt of his sword.

Chapter 11

I woke up spluttering. I gasped and coughed, trying to make sense out of whatever had happened to me. I felt steely fingers yank my face up, but my eyes would open no more than slits, and I was having trouble focusing. The hand pushed me away and I rolled over onto my back.

I tried to understand what had happened but nothing was coming to me. A fireball of agony erupted in my shoulder then, forcing my eyes wide in spite of the pain of sensory overload. I was in a…I had no idea where I was. Stone walls surrounded me; the type made with block and mortar not poured concrete. There were torches set in sconces in the wall and various metal devices and ropes around the room that did not look promising.

Most important at the moment was the man above me who had a boot on my chest and his hand wrapped around the crossbow bolt in my shoulder. He gave it another twist and I gasped, feeling the pain turn something inside me. I felt my muscles tighten and my fists clench at my sides. My nails dug into my palms as the rage began to wash through me.

"Meenos, enough!"

The man backed away and I was left glaring at him, my chest heaving with breath. Behind him was the man who had spoken. He was older, by far, but still looked powerful and dangerous. What was most disturbing about him, though, was just how familiar he looked.

"Welcome to my world," he said with a sinister grin. "You've done better than I ever would have hoped in siring that young witch. She's a powerful girl. With proper training I'll have this world and yours in my hand!"

"Who are you?" I gasped, trying to sit up.

"Look closely," he said, walking towards me and leaning over me. I studied him through the waves of nausea. He was very familiar, but I could not place him. He had a strong jaw line, blue eyes, and hair that had once been dark, but was now shot through with white. A scar on one jaw, faded from years of healing, completed his look. I suspected he was Lord Baxter, but the icy dread that filled my stomach hinted at further suspicions I dare not think through.

Seeing my lack of comprehension, he sighed. He turned and walked away, still speaking. "I am Vos Baxter, Lord of these lands. Ride a dozen days in any direction and still you'll still be in my realm.

"Baxter," he repeated with that smile. "The name of the man who tamed these lands, six generations past. The title of Lord has been passed down ever since to the most fitting heir. It's your name too, your daughter tells me." Rather than let me dwell on that, he changed topics quickly, keeping me off balance mentally and emotionally so that I was in the same shape as I felt physically. "It is a small realm by your standard, Mundling," he said, waving a hand, "but we do not use things such as you do. Science and technology have no place here. We thrive on hard work and divine guidance. Your ways are sinful and you will all be punished when I use the bridge to take over your world."

I wanted to laugh at him. The thought of a bunch of guys with clubs and bows fighting against Marines with tanks and helicopters struck me as ridiculous. Unfortunately, my sense of humor was mysteriously absent while I tried to come to terms with what he was telling me. Up until this moment I had forced myself not to think about it but now I had no choice. I knew that my mother had given me my father's name. And that she had sworn up and down that he would be back for us, even though he left her before she knew she was pregnant. He never returned however, but she refused to her dying day to accept that it could have been because he did not care for us.

He grinned at me while he saw me trying to process everything he said. "You've figured it out then?"

I nodded, just slightly. I didn't know what else to do.

"Good!" he said with a clap and a laugh. "Then perhaps you can answer a question for me! I wondered, which one was your mother?" I stared at him, not understanding. "There were so many. A month with the whores of your world. There must have been a dozen of them, maybe more?" He sighed for effect while I fought to keep myself from comparing what he said to the things my mother had claimed. It was no use, even though I knew he was waging a psychological war against me. "I should expect as much, they're not much better than the women here," he added as an afterthought. "Here at least they know their place and should they forget it, it's every man's responsibility to remind them."

My physical nausea was nothing compared to the sickness his words induced in me. I wanted to hit him, to break his jaw with anything I could find just to stop the nonsense he was spouting. It was more than the insult to my mother, it was the insult to all women. Some were lousy, perhaps, just as some men were, but others were kind and sweet and beyond reproach. Women like Krystan, for example. She deserved none of the filth he was describing, but if she were to stand up for herself and throw off her disguise, she'd be beaten and raped. And Lord Baxter would call that justice.

The mirth in his expression showed that he saw the effect on my face that his words had on me. His eyes twinkled. Then, finally, he went to a door and opened it. He spoke through the open doorway, his words muffled and echoing so I could not understand him. A moment later he returned, with Jessica in tow.

"Jess!" I hissed, trying to rise up again. The jailor, Meenos, put his boot to my chest and pushed me down.

"Daddy!" she screamed, trying to run to me. Vos grabbed her shoulder, his fingers pinching in cruelly, and held her back.

"This is why you're going to do what I tell you," he told her, wrapping his fingers around her neck and making her stare at me. "Your daddy is a lot harder to kill since he disposed of my best hunter, but don't worry, I have the means. And besides," he added with a smirk, "this way he can endure more pain if you displease me."

On cue, Meenos grabbed the bolt and gave it a slight tug. I gasped in pain in spite of my resolve not to. The only thing that amazed me other than the pain was the lack of blood from the wound.

"And this," he said, looking up at me and giving her a little shake as well, "will keep you in line. At any given time an archer, witch, or a wizard will have her in his sights. Try to use your newfound strength in a way that displeases me..."

Jessica cried out as he squeezed her neck. I started to push myself up against the boot of my jailer, but stopped when Vos relinquished his grip. He pulled Jessica away from me, towards the door. "Clean him up and have him brought to me, I want to keep an eye on both of them."

The door shut behind him and Meenos chuckled. He reached down to the bolt again. I gritted my teeth and wondered if I could knock him down, but before I could think to act, he wrapped his fingers around it and pulled. Hard. I screamed as he tore the barbed point out of my flesh, passing out from the pain it caused.

* * * *

I awoke as my father's hostage. He was a tyrant of the sort that seemed unmatched in my own memories of high school history class. He oppressed his people every minute of the day, seldom offering reward or praise. Instead he enforced and encouraged a kind of law that mocked any notion of real justice.

I seldom saw Jessica, and whenever either of us tried to speak to each other, we were punished severely for it. He took particular delight in seeing our torment. I vowed a thousand times by the end of the first day that I would make him pay for the damage he was doing to her. What happened to me no longer mattered, I focused only on trying to find a way to improve her life.

Finding my options limited, I set to learning as much as I could about Lord Baxter and the world we had stumbled on to. Twice a day, at dawn and dusk, devotions occurred. Every man, women, and child was required to stop whatever they were doing and face the castle. They dropped to a knee and silently prayed to Lord Baxter, asking his guidance in all things and forgiveness for their weak ways. I was sickened the first time I saw it, and only after I lost count of the days that we'd been imprisoned was I growing accustomed to it, though I still found it morally offensive. I learned early on that I had to participate in the devotions as well. Resistance only brought enforced obedience by my torturers or the knowledge that Jessica would be abused until I complied. On my third day I was beaten badly for no reason. Through the flogging I saw Jessica being forced to watch until she agreed to take part in the ritual. Apparently the rules were similar for both of us: we were being held hostage against one another.

Vos saw to it that I was trained in other ways as well. One day, less than a week after my capture, he turned to where I stood while he held court. He was between petitioners and said, "I'm told you fought poorly against my guard. Yet somehow you defeated my huntsman. If you are to replace him, you must learn how to fight."

"I'm not going to replace anyone," I said, my spirit unbroken in spite of the soreness in my back and legs from standing for so long. I still had hopes of Vos making a mistake. Leaving me and Jessica alone together or at least close enough that I could find a way to grab her and run. My small room was guarded at night and the door locked, I suspected hers was the same. Still, I had nowhere to go without her, so I could bide my time. What I would not do was help him.

He chuckled, belittling my silent resolutions. "So you say," he said, then turned to the next merchant that bowed before him.

This merchant was lodging a complaint against a rival merchant for not supplying him with the lumber he needed at a price he could afford to build and sell his carts. Vos' resolution involved taxing both men based upon the price. The higher the selling price, the more they would both pay. The merchant went away mollified, but distressed as he realized he would have been better off to have just paid the higher price. Now he would have a furious supplier as well as a cost that would be the same with the new tax.

I'd presumed that my answer had been the end of the matter, but after Lord Baxter had finished with the merchant, he turned back to me. "If you'd prefer I could have Jessica trained for the job instead?"

I glared at him and he laughed. He knew he had won.

At first I thought it might just be an excuse for more abuse. Later that day I was taken into a large room filled with seats around the edges. The floor was bare stone, which I later learned made it easier to clean up. Vos and a few others moved to occupy seats. Refreshments were brought in and then a servant came in and offered me a wooden stick. It was a little longer than my arm and roughly an inch thick. Far from a dowel produced on a lathe, it was at least straight and lacking any obvious bumps or irregularities.

Another man entered, this one a guard. He wore the standard leather armor of Vos' soldiers, and wielded his own stick in place of a sword. I looked down at my own and then at his. They were matched, but I had no real idea on how to use it, nor did I have the benefit of any armor. Far from it: my shirt had been stripped from me and I stood there only in my boots and my pants.

I heard Jessica and I smelled her at the same time. Turning my head in response to her gasp, I watched as Jess was led in by an old woman who looked like one of the evil matriarchs in a Disney film. She was Vos' oldest and most trusted witch. Also, she was one of the least gifted so she served to tutor other witches. That meant she was Jessica's trainer and jailer.

"Just in case you had any ideas," Vos said with a smirk, getting my attention.

I felt my lip curl up a little, but then he clapped his hands for us to begin. I turned back to the guard just as his stick jabbed into my stomach and made the air explode from my lungs. I stumbled backwards a few steps, my own stick held defensively in front of me while my other hand went to my belly protectively.

The guard was grinning. He advanced again and swung his stick. I tried to block it, and partially succeeded. His stick slammed into mine, jarring it in my hand, then his slid down the length and smashed into my knuckles. Breath hissed through my teeth and I dropped my stick, jumping back in pain. He pursued.

The stick came in again and again, and without my own for defense I did what I could to try and protect myself with my arms. He beat me repeatedly, jabbing into my chest and stomach or sides when he grew tired of leaving bruises and welts on my arms and head. It was agonizing and I wanted to curl into a ball until it was over.

Something inside of me twisted and rolled. It was an odd feeling, something that was not me, but yet somehow was. Through the haze of pain from the beatings I had trouble focusing on it. I just wanted it all to stop. I heard Jessica crying in the background, though I could barely understand it. Others were clapping, some laughing, and one, Vos, I think, was shouting at me. What he was saying I could not focus on.

I dwelt on Jessica mostly. Hearing her agony at seeing my pain infuriated me. The pain faded, replaced by numbness and a tingling feeling, as though my limbs had fallen asleep. I growled angrily and straightened up, accepting another strike to my side that landed with a resounding crack. Since his stick was unharmed, I could only guess my ribs had surrendered instead.

I trapped it against my side and twisted it away from him. Surprised, he hesitated, which gave me the chance to grab his stick and smash it over my knee into two pieces. I threw them off to the side, then, breathing heavily, I turned away from him to look at the suddenly silent audience.

"Daddy!" Jessica gasped in warning.

Too late, I tried to turn back. My opponent had grabbed my fallen stick and swung it at me instead. It cracked in the back of my head and my last memory was of a falling sensation that turned into blackness.

When I awoke only a few people remained in the room. Vos knelt down beside me as my eyelids fluttered open. I could taste blood in my mouth and my entire body ached. I had the most paralyzing headache I had ever experienced.

"You're a terrible fighter," he stated. "You had an advantage, though a man with a sword would have cut you to pieces long before that. Always fight, and never let up. Grant no quarter, for none will be given." He stood up. He turned to some of the servants and spoke, though his final comments were rhetorical. "Enough. Clean him up, we'll see if he learned anything from this tomorrow."

Tomorrow? That meant Baxter expected me to do this again. I half expected them to start taking bets on me. Not on whether I would win, but on how long it would take until I was beaten into a coma.

I groaned as servants helped me to my feet. Or, more accurately, they picked me up. I had been healing quickly, especially with the larger and more regular meals I had been eating. The one thing I would admit that was far superior here to on my world was the food. All organic natural food, no pesticides, no microwaved processed junk. I had been eating ravenously and in spite of it, I seemed to be getting leaner and stronger.

Twice a day I was given a different opponent. Mostly they beat me soundly and I ended up in agony, but I learned slowly how to fight back. It hurt and it infuriated me, but I was a captive at the whim of my captor. At least Jessica no longer had to watch the brutality I was forced to endure.

While recovering from my training sessions I watched Vos conduct court. Always, he took a cut of everything and ruled in favor of what benefited him the most, rather than his subjects. I only had a single opportunity to see him discuss the portal to my world, however. It involved negotiations with a neighboring tyrant, but no matter how hard I tried to focus on it I had trouble doing so thanks to a brutal blow to my jaw earlier that had left my teeth loose and my head swimming. I did gather that Vos meant to gain favor by allowing others to use his portal, but some of the phrases they used were beyond me. I also wondered what those others might gain from it. Magic or not, Vos and his peers didn't have enough men or technology to stand a hope against the United States army.

As before, I always healed. Instead of a blessing I began to see it as a curse. It meant Vos could have me beaten and abused that much more thoroughly.

One day, a few weeks after I arrived, Vos took me with him when he went out to hunt. There were others with us, but they were there for security and as reminders that I was to behave. Jessica was held captive, I needed no other reminder.

"We hunt bear today," he said, fitting a bolt to a mighty crossbow and cranking it back. "My rangers have tracked one in this area."

I waited, wondering why he was bothering to explain himself. Somebody, one of the guards behind me, grabbed my shirt and yanked me off my horse without warning. I fell to the ground painfully and growled, then slowly stood up. I looked up at his horse and at him, which was right in front of me. The horse whinnied nervously and backed away in spite of the guard cursing and trying to reign it in. The others laughed, either at my fate or at his inability to calm his mount, I did not know.

"Find him and bring him to me," Vos said after he stopped chuckling.

I looked at him, not comprehending immediately. "The bear? I'm a fisherman, I can put you on a fine school of whitefish, but I'm no hunter."

He laughed again cruelly. "Oh but you are. You killed Bodrik, my finest hunter. I have heard and seen it myself: you took the hunter inside you when you did it. I don't know how you managed it, since you'd still be bested by a nursemaid with a towel in a fight, but you're getting better."

He meant the wolf. My sense of smell and strength and, it seemed, how quickly I healed. The crossbow bolt had hurt badly, but it had not bled. When it came out the wound was fine in minutes. Likewise in a matter of hours between my daily beatings I was ready for the next session. That hardly stopped me from feeling a mix of fear and of anger.

"You don't understand yet, do you?" he asked, clearly enjoying himself. "Bodrik was your brother in many ways. Not just my son, but he was a changeling too. When he was a babe he was joined with the spirit of a wolf cub. An elaborate ritual that was very dangerous for him and for those involved." He leaned towards me and growled, "It cost me a lot of money and left my finest witch useless for weeks!"

"All right, I'll see if I can find it," I said through gritted teeth. I had no desire to hear how else he valued his son that I had killed.

"Don't harm it, son," he said, changing his mannerism like a man hosting multiple personalities. Then again, he enjoyed keeping those around him off balance and not knowing what to expect. He knew how much I hated him and that I hated him being my father even more. "And don't think to run off, I have darling little Jessica still."

Hands clenched and nails digging into my palms, I set off into the woods, away from the trail and into the bush. I slowly gave myself over to my senses, listening and smelling the woods around me. Just like at home, the forest was coming alive as Spring wore on. Leaves were unfurling and the fresh shoots of vegetation were climbing to the sky. In any other situation, I would have paused to enjoy the natural beauty of it.

My situation did not warrant such relaxation, however. I had stopped marveling at my new senses almost as quickly as I came to understand them. The faintest of smells could be harsh to me now, and given the lack of technology and personal hygiene found amongst the common folk, it really was a curse more often than a blessing.

In a while I managed to get the stink of the guards out of my nose. I felt the faint wind that made its way through the trees and really began to understand the power I had inherited from Bodrik. Our blood had mixed when we fought, and each time he had shared more and more of the magic that had created him with me. I had no idea what my limits were, but I also had little interest in finding them if doing so would make me like he was.

I growled at the thought of what he was; a hunter that had stolen my little girl from me. I felt that pain in my palms again and forced myself to stop and breathe, relaxing myself slightly. When I felt the tension in my shoulders release, I began searching about again, wondering how I might find this bear and, even if I managed, how I could bring it back to Vos.

The geography of the Dark Earth was similar to my own world, but roads and cities were different. Anything man made, for that matter, seemed to be either missing or only a resemblance by pure chance. It was that lack of familiar structures, roads, and settlements that left me clueless as to my location. I could have been in my backyard, but without the road and the trees I had removed, and others I had planted as landmarks, I had no idea.

Directions I still had though. There was no way to stop a veteran sailor from being able to tell North from South and East from West. Even on land I had experience enough in these woods to never truly be lost. The wind came from the North and the West, much like in my own world, and on it I caught some unfamiliar scents that confused me.

Pausing, I tested the air, sniffing and tasting it and trying to sort out the different flavors. It confused me, but I knew some of them. Unwashed bodies, for example-there is nothing like the odors a man puts off when he's gone too long without a shower.

Curious and having no better lead, I headed upwind to see what I could. I moved swiftly, finding myself more sure footed than ever as I made my way through trees, brambles, and undergrowth fit to slow even the most agile of rabbits. I felt something within me, something predatory, and I knew it was the spirit of the hunter that lingered on in me. It filled me with a sense of wonder and joy, and not with the darkness I had expected.

I stepped lightly across the stones of a stream and wondered which one it might be called on my world. It was broad enough that it might be the Yellow Dog or Big Pup, but with no proper frame of reference I had no way of knowing. Suddenly, to the left of me, a snapping twig and a muffled intake of breath preceded some loose stones bouncing off of a rock wall and then plopping into the quickly rushing water below.

I crouched down, my thoughts forgotten, and I watched as a figure picked himself up from where he had slipped. I looked about, studying carefully, and picked out other shapes that had frozen while the lead man regained his footing. They had not seen me, but they would have soon had I not taken cover. I shook my head and felt a rush of anger for my carelessness.

I was about to turn away when something made me stay and take another look at them. They were dressed for war, I realized, yet instead of sporting large weapons and heavy metal armor, they had short blades and axes and these were wrapped tightly to their bodies and padded where necessary to prevent noise. Their armor was darkened leathers and hides that fit them well, reducing noise as well at the sake of protection. My eyes narrowed, these men were not Lord Baxter's. Either he had led me off his lands, which seemed unlikely given his boast of the land for many days ride belonging to him, or these were raiders.

I slipped away carefully, stepping across some rocks and even walking a short distance in the frigid spring water before I made my way across the stream to the side towards which they were heading. They crossed on a log high above the stream, a place I could have easily beaten them to and defended even if only by tossing rocks at them and knocking them a dozen feet below to the rocky and shallow riverbed. But instead I watched, wondering what they were up to and also beginning to wonder if I could use them to my advantage.

Fresh smells came to me, warning me ahead of time. Turning I saw another group behind me, parallel to the first but a few hundred yards distant. Anywhere but the stream and they would have been undetected in the thick forest. I frowned, wondering what was going on. If there were two groups of men then surely more would be coming as well. I sniffed again and only now recognized the final strange smell: it was the smell of freshly oiled swords and axes.

I felt a twinge of anxiety, then fear. I was not concerned about myself so much; I knew I could get away. I was worried that perhaps they might be more than a simple raiding party. Perhaps war was coming and Lord Baxter was about to have his lands stripped from him. While that thought pleased me, what they might do to Jessica when they found her did not. As much as I did not wish to do so, I knew I needed to get back and warn him.

I slipped through the woods quietly but quickly. Branches and leaves rustled in my passing, but I heard no cry of alarm or sign of pursuit. Finding my way back was simple, which surprised me since I had not thought to mark any of the signs I passed as I left them. I stopped short of the trail they were on, my senses alerting me to trouble. The pained breathing of a horse; the wet hacking of a man's cough; and the smell of blood and flesh that had been spilt.

A fresh burst of adrenaline tore through my system and made me practically fly across the forest floor and burst out into the tall grasses that separated the horse trail from the forest. I saw a scene of desolation; of men and horses cut and split and left to die. I paused to recognize several of Vos' guards among the dead. A few other men, dressed like those I had seen, littered the ground as well. I did not see Vos, which caused my hope to soar and my pulse to relax slightly.

A cry from nearby and the clang of metal against metal caused my heart to hammer anew. I scooped up a fallen axe from the unfeeling fingers of an invader's corpse and ran through the brush. My run was brief. I followed the obvious tracks of men through a stand of elms and found three men standing with their backs to a moss covered rock. Five others gave battle to them, though one held back and was fitting a fresh arrow to a bow that reminded me of the compound bow I used for hunting, save it lacked any cams or wheels. Instead it was just a shortened recurved bow.

The curse I had heard a moment ago was from one of Lord Baxter's guards. He had an arrow sticking out of his stomach. A killing wound, I knew, given the technological backwater the Dark Earth was. I gripped the axe tightly in my hand and yelled hoarsely as I charge from behind. They turned, all of them, surprised to hear and see me. The attacker with the bow loosed his arrow and I distantly felt it hit me in the chest, though on my left side and near the edge.

I hacked the axe through the poor attempt at defense the first attacker made. He fell, the weapon stuck in between his shoulder and neck. I tried to keep my grip on it but it slipped from my fingers. I growled and felt a strange sensation in my chest.

Every breath I took, air hissed out around the arrow; it had punctured my lung. No blood ran from my wound though, which reassured me whatever curse I had acquired would protect me from death yet again.

The two guards and Vos himself rushed forward, striking into the backs of the attackers. I punched and scratched, feeling the sting of steel a few times but the adrenaline in me helped me to fight through the pain of it. In a few minutes they lay on the ground, dead. My chest was heaving with the effort to breathe, air escaping with every tortured gasp I took. One of my father's guards was dead as well, and the one with the arrow in his belly was leaning against the rock, a waxy pallor coloring his face. Vos, aside from a few scratches, was uninjured.

I reached up to the arrow in my chest and grasped it. It made me growl in pain as I did so, but that initiated a fresh surge of adrenaline as well. I yanked on it, as hard as I could, and heard myself try to howl in agony, but it came out as a tortured groan and a hiss of escaping air.

When the colors and spots stopped dancing in my eyes I found myself on my knees on the ground. Clenched in my fist I held the barbed arrow. I looked at it, swaying a little on my knees, and then I shook my head to try and refocus. I climbed to my feet, the hole already healing enough to prevent my lung from collapsing, and tossed the arrow to the ground.

"Do you see what you are now?" Vos asked me from behind.

I looked down at myself and saw the cuts in my clothing. I wore the clothing sewn and made from the hides of animals and other natural fibers that had been given to me by Vos. I had cuts on my arms and my side, but the wounds were healing at a supernatural rate. It seemed slow to me, but I knew in an hour or two I would have fresh scars and little more.

I turned to face him and saw he had an excited expression upon his face. “Look at your hands, Eric. Look at your enemies. Our enemies.”

I turned my hand and looked at them. There was blood on them, most especially my fingers. My eyes, horror struck at the realization, went to the bodies of the fallen. Two of them had scratches on them. Not simple scratches, but great gouges in their skin made not by simple human fingers, but by claws.

“I’m a monster,” I whispered, suddenly nauseous.

“Not a monster,” he said, “an instrument of power. Power I gave you!”

“You tried to kill me and steal my daughter,” I said, focusing angrily on him. I was back to wanting to strangle him myself.

Vos waved the comment away. “I needed Jessica, you were never a target.” My glare and clenching fists did not relent. “ You did what you must because you are a fighter. You are a warder,” he added. Seeing my recognition and surprise at the word he quickly pursued it. “Yes, you know what it means to be a warder. A protector. You are hers, I see it clearly. Even now, so far from her, you struggle to protect her.

“Join with me, Eric,” he continued. “It is foolish that we should be enemies. You are my son, you should not be my prisoner. Protect her and convince her to work with me. Together we will keep her from harm and crush those who would see us in ruin!”

"I will protect her," I told him, glancing down at my hands and forcing myself to relax. I could see how my hands had changed. They were hairier and the fingers longer. My fingernails had grown thicker and turned into short but sharp claws. As I relaxed, before my very eyes, they returned to what I was accustomed to. "I will never work with you," I finished, looking back up at him.

He shook his head, looking disappointed. "It's a long walk to the castle, son, we'd best be on our way."

I glared at him again as he turned away. Dark thoughts paraded through my head about the things I would like to do to him. I turned to look at the other guard and saw that he would never leave the rock he was leaning against. With a disgusted sigh I followed Lord Baxter as he headed back towards the castle. I thought of warning him of the other invaders that crept through the woods, but then darkly thought better of it.

Chapter 12

Vos found out soon enough that we were not alone in the woods. I could smell them first, but other than keeping my eyes peeled I showed no sign of it. Four arrows sped out of the woods on our left, preceded only half a heartbeat before by the muted twang of the bowstrings. Knowing they were close, I reacted in time and spun down and away. I heard the impact of another arrow and a curse, which told me that Vos was injured but alive.

I realized he might be hurt like his guard had been. Able to function for a while, but then afterwards he might succumb to his wounds. My stomach twisted at the thought and my nerves made me pay too little attention to the sound of people crashing out of the undergrowth to charge us. I barely reacted in time and rolled aside to dodge a sword point that dug a gouge in the ground.

"Dogs from Jascon," I heard Vos growl. He was already on his feet again. I saw him as I scrambled to my own. "Greet your Lord when I send him to meet you in Hell!"

I killed the attacker that was near me and managed to avoid any injury as well; I was getting better at putting my training to use. It would have disgusted and sickened me a few weeks ago. Now I was jaded to it; violence and force had become a constant in my life. It actually felt good to be on the giving end instead of the receiving end.

By the time I had finished my own disturbing realizations, Vos had slain three of the others and had the fourth preoccupied. I threw a short sword at him from behind, distracting him as it hit, and Vos finished him off. Vos bleed freely from the back of his head where the arrow had grazed him, but showed no other sign of injury.

"You must learn to fight better," he said to me as I came up to him. I scowled at him and he chuckled. "You're getting better–but you've a way to go. Come, there are many about, let's leave the path."

Having no say in the matter, I followed him as he led me through the forest. The bleeding had stopped on his scalp, but I could not help but want it to continue until he collapsed from it. I chastised myself for those thoughts because his survival was the only thing ensuring I would see Jessica alive again. Even so, my thoughts kept returning to the dark stain on his skin.

From Vos I learned more about my senses as well. I could smell fear and excitement coming from him. He was anxious about his castle and realm, though not for the people. I focused on that, rather than on reliving my own earlier moments of rage and action. I reasoned that I had done what I needed to at the time, and I would deal with the consequences of those actions later. The satisfaction and thrill I had felt had to be adrenaline. There was no other acceptable excuse for it.

Vos set a pace that would have left me gasping for breath only a month ago. Lord of the realm or not, he was familiar with his lands and no stranger to exercise. I could sense he was far from tired as well, even though by all accounts he was a man past his prime by more than a few years.

I knew we were close to another group of invaders and was about to warn Vos when he signaled me to silence. We slowed down and crept up to peer over a fallen log that was twice as wide as I was. Another group was working their way through the woods ahead of us, heading for Lord Baxter's castle. Vos gripped the sword at his side tightly and stood up. I reached out and grabbed his shoulder halting him. He glared at me murderously and I could see and smell his anger.

"We can go around them," I whispered. "Get back quicker."

"They invade my land," he said, eyes narrowing. "Do not be a coward, you could slay them all if you gave yourself over to the hunting."

He pulled away and I sat there stunned. I had never been called a coward before. That it was my biological father that did so was not important, it still stung my manly pride. I let it go and took a calming breath. All I had to do was remind myself that I came from a place that valued life more than death. Cowardice was not the problem here, it was the Dark Earth lack of respect for basic human life.

Vos burst around the log, moving quickly but somehow without making a sound. His sword plunged into the back of the last man in the troop, then he was among them, hacking and cutting his way through them. I wanted to let him fight them on his own, hopefully getting himself killed in the process, but then I remembered what—and who-was really at stake. With a grumble I leapt over the log and rushed to his side, just in time to help him dispatch the last two of the invaders.

He stood among them and looked at me, breathing hard but triumphant. "See this?" He held up his sword, which was red with the blood of the fallen. It was a straight blade over three feet long and three or four inches from one edge to the other. It looked like it was solid and durable, and while not pretty, the crosspiece, hilt, and even the base of the blade had some work put into them.

"This can kill you," he said, lowering the point menacingly at me.

"Do what you want with me," I spat back at him. I did not see the point for threats; he had established his dominance over me already. "I only care about Jessica."

He chuckled, turning the sound of laughter into something dark. "I'm not threatening you boy, I'm telling you that this sword is special, bewitched so it does not heal so easily when striking people like you. There are precious few around, and certainly not in the hands of common rabble like these."

I watched him kick the body of one of the men he had just killed. "You can die," he reminded me, "but it's no easy task. Drowning, burning, being torn apart by an animal or machine–those will kill you as dead as can be, but it takes a clever and sure strike with a common blade."

"It's not fear that holds me back," I retorted. "It's respect for life and the belief that those men have as much right to live as I do!"

"Even when they would just as soon gut you and have your daughter as their plaything?" he leered.

"Self-defense," I told him. "I do what I must to ensure her safety."

"Ever the warden. Come," he said, turning and swinging his sword through the air so that it whistled and blood flew from it. "We must return to my castle!"

We moved off again, sparing no time for discussions or debate. It was no simple trek either, despite his skill or my new talents. We ran into a few more bands of raiders, with Vos insisting on fighting each one along the way. I sported fresh wounds even while the old ones were healing. The trip had taken us nearly three hours by horse, and now we moved on foot. We were both tired, though both too proud to admit it to each other; we had been moving at a near jog for four hours and had stopped to fight multiple times. My only consolation was that I was getting much more familiar with how to handle myself in a fight. Watching Vos do battle left me more disconsolate, however, since I knew my strength and skill were no match for his.

We crossed over a river I strongly suspected was the dead river. It was far wider than I remembered it being, but in my world it had a dam and a storage basin upstream. The only way across involved wading and swimming, since Vos was insistent we should not use the bridge we had taken earlier. It was an easy crossing but the water was painfully cold, especially now that the evening was starting to wear on and the sun was no longer directly on us.

Scrambling up the far bank we were nearly turned into pincushions by arrows from the side we had just came from. Another squad of soldiers from the neighboring realm had seen us crossing and came to investigate. Vos turned to go after them but I tackled him, pulling him to the ground behind some trees. I felt like I had just tried to grapple with a statue his muscles were so hard and defined. His fist sent me reeling after we tumbled to a rest. Blinking back stars, I lunged and caught his leg, pulling him down. Arrows launched into the trees around us, but over our heads, fortunately.

"You want to fight them that's fine, wait till they cross!" I hissed at him as I dodged a kick from his semi-restrained foot. "You go out there now and you won't come close to crossing the river before they've stuck a dozen arrows in you!"

He wrenched his foot free of my grasp and lifted himself up enough to see over the bank and across the river. He hesitated, giving me a chance to crawl over as well. I saw them then, or at least the few that were at the edge of the trees. They had arrows nocked and were waiting for us.

"You want to throw your life away, fine, I'll be happy to help you," I growled at him. "But do it after Jessica is safe."

He backed away and, without any words, we slipped away from the river and continued towards his castle. After a few minutes he turned on me and grabbed my somewhat tattered shirt. "You were right," he acknowledged. "But do not ever lay a hand on me again or I will, in turn, lay a heavier hand on your precious daughter."

Somewhat frightened at first, his threat made me flush with anger instead. I opened my mouth to retort but he had pushed me away and turned around again by then. He started through the forest again, moving more carefully now for we were not so far from the town he called his home.

I was still going to retort when I caught the smell of smoke in the air. I hissed a warning to him, telling him of it, and a few moments later I saw him nod; he must have caught the scent as well. By then it was growing powerful to me, and I knew it came from the direction of the town and castle.

My legs were energized, in spite of the day's toils. I nearly passed Vos several times as we walked, despite the fact that he had sped up also. Coming upon small hills and rises we caught glimpses of the town under siege. A few buildings burned, though most stood unharmed. Few people moved in the streets, or at least few moved that did not do so quickly and fearfully. They darted from one building to another, seeking shelter or refuge. Others, invaders, moved more purposefully and sought to loot and pillage. My heart briefly leapt in my throat as I wondered how the smith fared. She faced trouble more than most, but I knew I had to put her from my mind if we were to survive this day.

Vos, seeing this, let out a angry grunt. He pushed on then, anxious to get there as quickly as possible. In another few minutes we were the ones moving through the deserted streets. We drew the attention of the enemy soldiers, but they fell before the enraged Vos with ease. Along the way I picked up another axe that had been dropped. I figured I was more dangerous with something I was somewhat familiar with compared to a sword, which I had never used before. Axes reminded me of oversized hatchets.

I did convince Vos to move through the shadows as the sun set, at least. He could not reclaim his lands if he were dead. Grudgingly, he switched back to moving stealthily as he had in the forest between fights. Still he seldom spoke; he was preoccupied with whatever thoughts were on his mind. I could only guess those thoughts involved vengeance and torture.

Finally we came to the gate, and there we saw a sight that filled me with terror. The gates were open, one of them burned badly and the other showing signs of being blackened on the outside, at least. I started forward, fearful for Jessica, but this time Vos held me back. Dozens, perhaps even hundreds, of invaders roamed through the gate. I could hear fighting inside so it seemed that all was not lost.

"Is there another way in?" I asked him, already looking around and trying to find some means of getting inside without using the occupied front gate.

"A few," he admitted. "None close though."

"There are archers on the walls still, a few, at least. Can we get one of them to toss a rope down to us?" I asked him, pointing up at one of the crossbowmen on the wall that was sniping into the crowd of aggressors.

"Too dark and too far, they'd not believe us," he said. "And if they did, Jascon's men would be on us ere we scaled the wall."

"It's your damned castle, how do we get in?" I hissed, glaring at him.

I saw that his expression was filled with steel. He may have been even angrier than I was at this intrusion, but he was as helpless to prevent it as I was.

"Seems you're not exactly in control of your realm and people right now," I said, feeling a moment of elation that perhaps I could throw off the yoke of slavery. "I'll help you get in, and help you with whatever you need to do inside, but only if you agree to help me get Jessica first."

"Don't think you have a choice," he growled at me.

"I do," I said. "I can leave you here right now, or maybe even call out to those men and tell them where you're hiding–in return I ask only to have her returned to me safely."

"They'd kill you beside me," he said. "And you don't know where to go if you ran for it."

"Seems we need each other then," I told him. "You could try it on your own," I said when he hesitated. "But you know better than I do what I can do. You know how helpful I can be. By yourself, strong or skilled as you are, they will wear you down and beat you."

A calculating look in his eye, he finally nodded. "So be it. Jascon employs men with special talents as well. Not so different from your own," he told me.

I shrugged. “I was just a fisherman when I killed your best hunter.”

He smirked in spite of our situation. “When they’ve been beaten back I think you and I may yet settle on good terms.”

“I wouldn’t take that bet if I were you,” I warned him, then turned to stare back out at the crowd. “Come, I have an idea!”

He followed me, for the first time, as I slipped away from the corner of the building we had been pressed against. A short prowl found me another squad of soldiers that had slipped out of the woods intending to join the sacking. I let them see me as I emerged from between buildings, then I turned and ran. They fell for it and immediately chased after me.

A few minutes later Vos and I were struggling into their armor, trying to pick pieces that fit the best. His sword he wrapped in his armor and carefully stashed amongst the still smoldering ruins of a burned out stable. I asked him about it, anxious for the time we lost, and he assured me that his blade was easily recognized and known far and wide. Wielding it would ruin the disguise.

We joined up with the throng at the gate, finding that most of the invaders had made their way in. We pushed through the crowd, easily blending in with the other soldiers, and I felt a moment of panic when I lost Vos at one point in the crowd. I had to ignore my vision for a moment, which saw only countless soldiers dressed in similar dark armor, and let my other senses sift through the chaos of stimulation. I found Vos’ scent and tracked him through the masses, emerging behind him on the edge of it. He led me towards a side door that led into a servants’ entrance into the keep.

The door was barred shut. Vos cursed and slammed his shoulder against it, causing it to shudder with each hit. It held firm, however, and in disgust he turned away from it. A few other invaders saw us and rushed over to see what we had found. I counted six of them, and was both cheered at the thought of help and concerned about the numbers against us. With their help we managed to break down the door. Doing so, however, exposed us to the retaliation of those inside.

Two of the attackers fell dead, stricken by bolts from crossbows. I staggered back myself, a chunk of flesh torn from my cheek from where one of their quarrels had struck my cheekbone a glancing blow and continued. It stung and I could only hope it would heal quickly. We were pushing inside then, Vos and I at the rear while the others yelled and charged the defending guardsmen.

The four remaining of Jascon's soldiers fell between us, and Vos's guards stared at us in confusion, for we had cut into their foes from behind. Vos tore off his helm and tossed it to the ground, revealing his identity to them. They relaxed at the sight of him, then jumped to come to my aid as I lost another axe into the forehead of an invader that tried to come to our aid from outside.

The door was propped back up and barred while Vos and I moved away from it with his sage advice of, "Hold that door better than you did against me or I'll have your heads and those of your firstborns on pikes!"

"You're not very good with people," I muttered to him as I followed him out of the kitchen and into the servant's corridors outside of it.

"This isn't like your world," he snapped back at me. "I lead because I am strong and they are weak. Give them the chance and they would be no better than the would-be butchers trying to ransack my keep!"

"Perhaps," I offered, walking briskly behind him. "Or perhaps your world could use a change. Maybe you need only to treat them well to see real loyalty instead of fear."

"Fear is better," he said over his shoulder to me; "it lasts longer than love."

"I've heard that before," I said, trying to pin it down. We came to a set of stairs and he took them three at a time, forcing me to do likewise.

"He was the last to come from my world to yours to stay," Vos said. "Machiavelli."

The name sounded familiar, but philosophy and history were not my strong points, so I let it drop. "You keep her up here?" I asked, changing the topic.

"Yes," he said, letting it drop in turn.

We turned down a hallway and went through a doorway into a very well equipped guard barracks. I recognized some of the standards on the shields and weapons that were still on racks as belonging to Vos' elite guard. I narrowed my eyes suspiciously and grabbed a long bladed knife off a table without Vos noticing.

"Hurry up and change," he said, already taking off the foreign armor he wore. "My men see you dressed like that and they'll strike first and ask questions later."

"What about Jess?" I asked, accusing him by my tone.

"She's guarded," he said. "And I made sure they are able to stop even you," he added.

No less doubting, I stripped off my stolen armor and found some that nearly fit me from his special guard. They wore padded shirts and leggings with metal rings threaded into them. I had seen suits of chain mail in movies, and this seemed similar, if a bit different. I had no idea what it actually was, but I found it not unbearable to wear in spite of it being rather heavy.

Vos helped me get it fitted properly since I was unfamiliar with it, then he led me through another door and into his audience hall. I had seen this before, and I found I was not surprised in spite of being furious at him for misleading me. Before I could call him out we were noticed by the various servants and guardsmen in the room.

"Lord Baxter, you've returned! We thought you were lost," his aide called out, rushing towards him.

"Hoped, more likely," Vos said. "I'll look into how Jascon's men can get to my city without any warning when this is over. When I find the source of that treachery I plan to personally flay the skin from that traitor and keep them alive to enjoy the punishment! Right now, I expect us to retake this town," he yelled, looking angrily about the room at everyone gathered. Already others were coming in, for word had spread from those who had seen us roaming the halls in our stolen garb.

"My daughter," I interrupted, angrily.

He turned to look at me while everyone else looked on in shock and surprise. "Your daughter is safe," he said curtly. "You will mind your tongue and do as I say or you may find her being used to distract our enemies."

"My Lord!" a messenger said, bursting into the room with blood running down his arm. I was spared any further attention thanks to that man. I let the dagger I had hidden up my sleeve slide into my palm and I could feel the cold steel pressing against my arm now that most of it was unsheathed.

"They've broken into the keep! We're fighting to hold them back, but there're too many of them!"

Vos looked apoplectic with rage. "Go! Kill them! Kill every last one and if I find any quarter given or anyone that turns tail, I will send my hunters to bring them back to me so I can kill them myself!" The messenger turned whiter than he already was, nodded, and turned to run off. Vos looked around the room and screamed again. "All of you! Arm yourselves and fight! What I promise you for failure is far less than the appreciation Jascon will show you!"

Stumbling over one another, the courtiers scrambled to get out. In a few minutes only Vos and I remained; even his aide had seen his fury and had left. Vos turned to me and shook his head. "Put it away boy," he said.

I bristled at being called a boy. It had been years since anyone had spoken to me so. I was sure he felt he was justified in doing so, he was my father even if I refused to acknowledge him as such. I let the dagger slide out further and gripped it in my hand, reversing it so the blade was point out.

"You lied to me."

"You're better now than you were," he said calmly, "but you're nowhere near good enough. Put that knife away and you might get to see young Jessica again."

"You've lost," I told him. "You don't have enough men left to stop them, and I've seen some of those men before. Your men have deserted. They're wearing Jascon's colors, that's why you had no warning."

His nostrils flared and I knew how close he was to lashing out at me. A man in a coma would have known how dangerous Vos was at that very moment. I pulled out the sheath from where it was tucked up my sleeve and slid the knife into it. "Killing you won't help me anymore," I told him, then I turned away.

He roared and launched himself at me. I spun away from him but still felt his hand grab at the hem of my shirt and jerk me around. I tried to tear myself free, telling myself that the pain in my throat would heal. He wrapped his arm around me and I felt the cold sting of steel at my throat.

"I cut your throat from ear to ear and you'll not be able to heal fast enough," he hissed at me.

"What good does killing me do you?" I asked him, feeling the keen edge slicing through my skin with every movement of my jaw. "If you stop we can get Jess and be away before your castle falls," I continued. "Escape to live and you can fight another day; You can have the vengeance you crave."

He pushed me away roughly. "I'll not underestimate you again," he said, then he barked a short laugh. "You came from my loins, I was foolish to have ever doubted. Which one was your mother?" he asked again, even as he turned to head towards a door to his private offices. "I bedded nearly a score while I visited your world."

I knew he was trying to get to me, and it was working. My mom had done nothing great in her life, but she was still my mom and had earned my respect and love. Times had been tough and she had not always made the best decisions, but we'd found our way through them together. At least she had never abandoned me as he had. I would not give him the satisfaction of answering him.

"Let her go and I'll help you," I said.

He stopped and laughed. "You're a fool," he said. "I don't care about her anymore. She was a key to open a doorway, that's all. Now that it's open already I've sent people through to establish themselves. Including some of my own witches.

"The bridge is open, they'll be unrestricted over there even if she returns to your world," he said vindictively. He began walking again and I followed, a lump in my throat at the thought of my world tainted with the kind of evil I had found in this one.

"That's why you're being overrun then, isn't it?" I asked him.

He shrugged. "Perhaps. I gambled and sent too many loyal men through the bridge. Somehow my neighbors found out and they want the bridge for themselves."

"Can it be closed?" I asked him.

"You'd have to send every gifted back to their own world or kill them where they are. Already there are witches moving through your world to different areas, trying to open bridges back to their own realms."

"What?" I asked, not understanding him on one hand and afraid that I understood him too well on the other.

"I made deals with other Lords of distant realms," he said. "They sent their gifted to me to assist, and in return once it was open they were to go through and seek to create a portal for their own realm." I swore, lacking any better response. Vos barked another dark chuckle at my concern. "What good will your weapons be when their enemies are among them?"

"Where is she?" I growled at him, unable and unwilling to continue the conversation. My sanity and conscience rested solely on the safe recovery of my daughter.

He pointed down the hallway. "Those stairs lead up to the final floor. She's being kept in a guest room. Go right ahead."

"You said she's guarded."

He shrugged. "I did, but there's no telling whether those guards are loyal or not now."

"Lead the way then," I said. It seemed as if I was taking control of things, but I suspected he was only letting me believe that. He had years of experience at being duplicitous and dominant, after all.

He started down the hallway but then, at the other end, we saw a group of Jascon's men round a corner and shout when they saw us. They launched in a run, heading our way. I judged the distance and realized that if they were that close, they might already be on the next floor up as well. I launched into a run of my own and headed toward the stairs.

I had to stop short when I found two men coming down the stairs. I backed up as they gave a shout and came at me. I barely had my knife out in time to blow the first slice of a short sword. Vos stepped past me and intercepted the other four coming at us.

Lacking the skill to properly fence, I accepted a stinging blow along my ribs so I could get in close and rip my knife into the man's belly. My armor stopped the sword from cutting, but my ribs still ached for a moment from the impact of the blade. I kept my adversary between myself and the other man, foiling his attempts to get at me. My first foe slumped to the ground, defeated, and I had to hurry to dodge back and duck the attack from the other.

He was a little more cautious as he approached me. That prompted me to be less cautious. I stepped into him, thrusting wildly and accepting how easily he knocked my knife aside. He was not prepared for my next attack though, it was my hand, fingers and claws extended as it tore across his face. He screamed as he fell, clutching at his injuries. My dagger silenced him forever.

Vos, still fighting, spared a brief glance that cost him a stinging slap against his forearm. I watched him for a brief moment and then opted to sprint up the stairs for Jessica. By the time I cleared the top step I heard the gasp of winded agony from Vos' last opponent. I knew he would be behind me soon.

I turned down the hall, looking in both directions. Several doors were opened with various things strewn about the hall way. Shreds of cloth in some places, a plant and broken clay urn in another. I saw bodies as well, some from servants of either gender, and some of invaders and defenders. The latter drew me like a moth to a flame.

The room was abandoned. I saw one of Vos' elite guards inside, dead from injuries received. Three attackers lay around him, equally slain. There was no sign of anyone else in the room. I could smell her though, amidst the stink of sweat and death. Her sweet aroma lingered still.

I walked woodenly to the large bed in the room and reached for the pillow. I saw how bloodied my hand was but I did not care. I pulled the pillow to my face and inhaled deeply, drawing in her scent and filling myself with it. I remembered pleasant times for a few eternal seconds. Playing in the forest back in our world. Sharing time while helping her with homework. Listening to her read a poem she had written to me.

I dropped the pillow and howled. It was meant as a scream of rage and pain, but it came out a howl not so unlike that of the noise Jess and I had heard in our cabin before Bodrik had attacked us. She had been taken. I had failed her again.

"Yes," Vos hissed behind me, urging me on. "Give in to it. Become the hunter. You have her scent, now track her down and let nothing stop you."

I turned to see him, not even recognizing him at the moment. The knife fell from my hands, which were cramped with the change they were caught up in. Dark fur covered the back of my hands and my fingernails were hooked and cruel looking claws. I could feel my teeth protruding against my gums as well, and running my tongue against them I felt the sharpness of their points.

"Lead the way, my son, and let us hunt!"

I broke into a jog and left the room behind me, my body turning to face the direction where I knew her scent to be heading. Beyond that my memory is blurred of the chase through the keep. I know I ran through the manor, tracking Jessica's scent. I know I encountered others, some of them defenders and some attackers. I did not care who they were, if they were in my way they fell before me. I did know that Vos followed me. I could smell him and hear him. He alone was safe in my company so long as he was an ally and not a foe.

I left the keep behind and tore through the confused ranks of attackers in the courtyard. A cry went up and they ran, clearly seeing I was no simple man they could easily defeat. I had no idea what I looked like, I just felt the beast inside of me straining to get out. I let it have nearly free reign, contorting my face and limbs as I raced after my daughter.

I identified the smells of those that had captured her as well, they were different than the normal scent of men. Some distant part of me wondered why that was, but my mind was given to instinct and hunger for the hunt, so it remained an unanswered question. Unanswered until that very moment, however.

A lone man stood in my path. Jessica's scent was getting stronger, driving me after her with renewed fury. This new obstacle I could tell was different, but he remained an obstacle that I merely needed to overcome. An inconvenience like a speed bump, as far as I was concerned.

He changed as I raced at him. I expected to crash into him, ripping him to shreds as I did so, and then move on. What I saw caused my body to change its strategy even as I wondered what was going on. The hunter within me knew what to do, though I did not. Already a large man, he thickened and flexed, his own hands becoming hairy and sprouting thick claws. His face elongated, his beard and mustache growing longer and resembling fur. In moments I realized I faced something not so different from what I had become, save that he had the spirit of a bear for a companion instead of a wolf.

We collided in an explosion of hair and claws. He caught me even as I slashed at his chest and face, throwing me aside easily. I rolled to my feet easily, the scratches he had given me starting to heal already. Likewise I saw the wounds I had inflicted on him recovering before my very eyes. It seemed the more I gave myself up to the hunter inside, the quicker I recovered. Apparently others inflicted with similar conditions behaved similarly.

The bear-man roared at me. I wasted no time in responding, but lunged at him again. I danced around, dodging a powerful swing aimed at gutting me, and tore into his shoulder and side. He turned on me quicker than I expected, backhanding me and sending me skidding to the ground again. He was slower than I was, but stronger too.

We fought, me growing increasingly angry as time slipped past us. Neither of us could score a wound that was enough to signal defeat, though we both came close a few times. Time was not on my side, I knew. Either he would get help from the other invaders or Jessica would be beyond my reach. I slashed and bit at him, tasting fur and skin, but as always we parted ways with no real lasting damage.

"Hunt!"

I heard Vos from the crowd. He had managed to find himself a secluded spot to watch. Others were calling out so his single word drew no undue attention.

I turned it over in my mind, wondering what he could mean. The distraction nearly cost my life as my opponent staggered me with a swipe that tore rings and cloth from my shirt and left my ribs displayed to the world for a few painful moments. It occurred to me what I needed to do when I found my arm not responding properly. The muscles controlling some of my range of motion with it were shredded, temporarily. I danced away, circling even as my foe tried to press the advantage. I favored it, lips curled up and showing him teeth that would have made my dentist faint.

I let him close and let him land another blow, even as I was leaping away in the direction he was swinging. His clawed fist staggered me and blasted the air from my lungs, but it also propelled me in the direction I wanted to go.

I hit the ground and rolled, my arms already coming around. My fingernails, claws really, tore into his leg. I dug them in and tore them out, tearing muscle and flesh. He roared, his leg collapsing and nearly dropping him on top of me. His arms flailed out, hitting the ground in an effort to arrest his fall. I lunged at him and turned the threat Vos had given me earlier that night into a reality.

Blood sprayed into my face and onto his chest. He fell back, clutching at his neck and trying to stem the blood flow. I lost a moment, surprised. Thus far I had hardly shed a drop of blood and, fighting this man-bear thing, neither had he. The wound was serious, something possibly unrecoverable. Vos had taunted me with as much and now I began to understand.

He stared at me, realization in his eyes. He reached up but I jumped away just in time to avoid what was no doubt his attempt to drag me into death with him. I let him roll back and forth a moment then I slipped in, grabbed his head, and twisted it violently. The resounding crack was followed by his entire body spasming once, then it lay still.

I looked around, breathing heavily, and saw a stunned look on many faces. I snarled, my blood still up, and ran after my daughter's scent again. The soldiers that had begun to ring me tried to scatter away, but those that did not felt tooth and claw.

I had become the hunter. I felt exhilaration and power. I was unstoppable! I ran, lean and crouching low as an occasional arrow flew past me. I tasted Jessica's trail and I knew I would catch her. Nothing would stop me.

Nothing except a sudden fist the size of a building that slammed into me from above. I dropped to the ground, my senses reeling and my chest heaving for the breath that had been blasted from me. I tried to pick myself up, wondering what could have possibly hit me, but I found myself unable to move. I could feel my hands and legs, and there was no new pain. Still I was pinned as though a giant hand pressed upon me.

I turned my head, looking around, and saw people running towards me. One, in particular, drew my attention. It was a woman wearing a dark robe. Dresses on women were the standard here, but this was something that reminded me more of something

I would have expected to see in a fantasy movie. The necklace about her neck completed the look, it had the bones of various creatures laced into it. She was focusing on me, her hand out and palm face down, as though she was personally pushing against me.

Enraged, I struggled. I could move, a little, but I could not rise. I was surrounded shortly and men grabbed my arms, pulling them around and tying them behind my back. My legs were tied as well. I struggled, trying to lash out and at least injure my new captors. Eventually they tired of my struggles and drove me into unconsciousness with blunt strikes to my head.

Chapter 13

I woke to find myself bound and gagged and riding in a wagon. Riding is a strong term, tossed like a sack of flour would be more accurate. I shifted, contorting my body and managing to roll so that I could at last lift myself up enough to lean against the side of the four wheeled cart.

The moving cart was surrounded by men on horses and on foot. Guards, or soldiers, if there was a difference. Either way, they belonged to the enemy that had managed to overrun Vos's realm. Ahead I could only see riders and the trail, and behind more of the same. The trail, at least, looked recently built. The way the wagon rocked as it went over bumps and holes in the road reinforced my opinion of it.

I was seen as soon as I started to struggle to my feet. A few threats and jeers were tossed my way, but aside from that they left me alone. I let the day's events play back through my head and I felt my mood swing from fear of being caught to anger at my situation and Jessica's abduction and then finally to depression. I was captured again, and this time without even the hope of seeing my daughter. For all I knew they had killed her or worse. If they knew she was gifted there was no telling what horrors she might be subjected to.

Thinking of the gifted I turned my head to look around. Nowhere nearby did I see the witch that had been able to subdue me. I tested my bonds thoughtfully, but found them tied fast. I tried to find the spirit of the wolf within me so that I might shift and change, but whenever I came close it slipped through my fingers like sand clenched in a fist. I could not focus on it, every time I got angry the anger soon evaporated into despair.

It was dark out, at least. The moon was filling each night, but it seemed my condition had nothing to do with a full moon. According to Vos, I had somehow absorbed some or all of the same curse that Bodrik, my predecessor, had been given via some complicated magical ritual. The moon was irrelevant, other than that it had to be conducted on the night of a full moon.

Having killed the other changeling, I wondered if I had acquired some of his talents as well. Could I call on the spirit of a bear as well? I struggled to find some semblance of calm so I could search myself for some clue or hint or another spirit. I was denied, there was nothing but the hunter in me, and it was ignoring me presently. I slumped against the wagon defeated and exhausted.

Time passed, marked only by the lurches and bumps that drove my tailbone into the unforgiving wooden planks of the wagon. Soon enough we stopped and I roused myself from my depressed stupor to look around. I saw a clearing ahead, and that drew my interest more thoroughly. A light was streaming out from it, and it was not the flickering light that torches and campfires set off. Too many people were in the way but I could feel a tingle on my skin that told me there was something special about it.

A commotion ahead alerted me to something happening. A short while later I saw the crowd of soldiers parting to let some people through. One of these was the witch who had given me a technical knockout, and there were some others I did not recognize. One of them, a large man trailing behind her, I had a hunch was another one of Jascon's special forces; another man that shared the strength of a bear or perhaps something else. I had no idea why or how I knew this, but I was learning to trust my instincts, so I vowed to avoid him until my own head was in a better place.

The irony of me thinking about freedom and fighting was not lost on me. I found myself scowling at myself for being amused, then just let the emotions drain from me as they reached the wagon and looked up at me. I glared at them, daring them to make a move. They did not disappoint.

"I hear you came from Mundania," said one of the men. He wore the armor of a soldier, but his was of a finer quality. Aside from that, he was no more remarkable than any of the other men assembled. "I am Lord Jascon."

I stared at him, unimpressed. I looked away, my message clear to him. The large man beside him made a rumbling noise deep in his chest and moved so that he could grab my head in a single meaty fist and twist it back around so that I was staring at Jascon.

"Yes, I heard you were difficult," he said. "I know so little of Mundania, I was hoping you might be willing to educate me. Tell me, Mundling, is letting you live enough reward to earn your service?"

I tried to resist the hand that held me, but found the rest of my body shifting before my head did. I suspected that one of this guy's parents had mated with a bear, rather than just having a spirit trapped and joined with his. Unable to resist, I looked at Jascon and sneered at him. I would have spat, but my mouth was dry.

"What then?" he asked, sighing. "Name your price, I'm not the reckless sort that Baxter was. I won't risk sending my army and leaving myself defenseless as he did, nor will I send only a handful of men to be slaughtered."

My stomach flipped at the mention of Lord Baxter. As much as I loathed him, he suddenly seemed like a lifeline to me. We had spent a lot of time together and had fought beside each other. Were we allies? I had promised to help him if he helped me. Then again, he had betrayed me once already, why I would hope he might help this time around seemed to mark me as foolish.

"Let my daughter go," I told him.

"Ah, the witch that made this possible? The girl that was captured and came through?" He smiled and tapped his fingers against his cheek thoughtfully.

I found myself growling deep in my throat. Vos was cruel and a tyrant, but this man was all of that and petty as well.

"Bring him," he said, turning and walking back up towards the clearing.

I felt the big man's hands upon me, shifting and picking me up by the ropes that bound my hands and my feet. I was carried like a bale of hay, my teeth gritted against the tortured pain in my shoulders. He took little care in making sure I did not bounce off of horses, men, and other wagons and obstacles along the way. By the time I arrived at my destination I had a growing headache and a unbridled amount of anger within me. He dropped me on the ground and moved away, grinning with amusement at my plight. Jascon walked behind a small defensive wall set up in front of whatever was shedding off light. His witch stood nearby, staring at me and ignoring the raven that circled down out of the sky and landed on her shoulder.

"I'm going to kill you," I said, refocusing on the large man, my eyes narrowed into slits. I reveled in the momentary shock in his expression, even though he replaced it with a chuckle of amusement at my boast.

Inside I found myself recoiling. What had I just said? What was I becoming? This spirit, this hunter, was it infecting my mind as well as my body? Was I losing myself and becoming like the natives of this world?

Further thoughts were stripped from me when I heard a cry that was a cross between a gasp and a whimper. I recognized it, of course, and suddenly felt myself drowning in Jessica's scent. It had been there all along, but I had gotten accustomed to it and had not paid any attention. Now I felt as though there was no other smell in the world, or at least none so sweet.

"Release her?" he asked, stepping around a wooden barricade that had been erected.

He pulled Jessica with him, she was dressed in a robe, much like his own witch and those that Baxter's had worn. She looked strange to me, as though she was not herself. She hated dresses, always wanting to wear jeans or shorts. Perhaps that was why, or perhaps something about her had changed. It had only been a few days since I had seen her last, but she looked taller, somehow.

"Jess!" I gasped, my fury fleeing from me faster than water falling from the sky.

"Daddy!"

"I'll never understand you Mundlings," Jascon muttered, shaking his head.

"Tell me, hunter, what will you do if I release her?" he asked, teasing both of us and enjoying himself. The bear-man nearby chuckled as well. Jascon's witch, I noticed, showed no reaction.

"What do you want?" I asked him, rolling myself over so that I could sit up and lean against a tree stump. "Someone to teach you of my world?"

"For starters," he said, absentmindedly running his fingers through Jessica's tangled brown hair. It had been a trying day for her too, I could see.

"I've never had a wolf before. I might like having one of Baxter's prized hunters to serve me," he said.

I growled in spite of myself. "I never served him," I said.

"Oh? My spies tell me otherwise." He said thoughtfully. "Perhaps instead I will hold this witch as my guest, ensuring your good behavior."

I felt a burst of strength surge through me. The hunter seemed closer again. I could feel him, trying to reach me. I looked around, wondering what was wrong. I had only been cursed for a short time, but I had never had any trouble in calling it forth to serve me.

"Be careful, my Lord," his witch hissed. "He wears at my control as he grows angry. Make your deal or kill them–you have no need of the girl."

The witch. I glared at her, realizing she was the reason why I could not change. I had no idea how, but she was preventing the spirit of the wolf from joining with me. Even as I stared at her I could make out beads of perspiration on her forehead. I turned back to stare at Jascon, seeing how his hand rested none-too-innocently on Jessica's shoulders, his finger curled around her neck.

"Behind me is the portal to your world," he said, nodding his head towards it but not taking his eyes off of me nor his hand from Jessica. "You could go through it, but it would do you no good. Already the realm in which you live is overrun. Baxter's men started it, but now they will serve me."

"Witches travel through your world, seeking to open other gates. What good will it do you to flee?" he stated matter-of-factly. "Stay and serve me, and I promise you your daughter will be with you and have the run of my lands-escorted and protected, of course. She will be tutored as well, learning how to use her powers and to serve me well." He squeezed Jessica's neck meaningfully, making her squirm and whimper. "Resist and I will prove Carana right. I have no need of another witch, especially one so young. Nor do I have a need for you."

I stared, knowing I had no chance and hating it. I was ready to sell my soul but Jessica interrupted me.

"Please, leave him alone–I'll do what you want," she said.

I felt something breaking in my chest at hearing her words. She was giving up. I growled and pulled at my ropes, trying to break them. I desperately called out for the wolf, fighting against whatever restraints the witch used to separate it. The raven on her shoulder cawed and flapped its wings, as though it could feel her struggle.

I felt something else then too, something strange and furry. It brushed against my hands and nearly made me lose my concentration. A soft noise, a chattering sound, reached my ears and, combined with a familiar scent I had not noticed for weeks, I understood. It made no sense to me at all, but I was growing accustomed to that.

"It's not you I'm after," Jascon said with a chuckle. "Don't doubt I can't use you, but it's the novelty of your father that I'm most interested in. Of course you'll have to prove your worth. Bore me and I might have you both tortured and killed anyhow," he added as an afterthought.

The cracking knuckles of his head ruffian were an unspoken promise. I felt the rope around my wrists go slack. A nibble on the palm of my hand was the final confirmation and then my furry rescuer was gone.

"Well, wolfling, what say you?"

I raised my head defiantly. "We're better off dead than being your slaves."

He raised both eyebrows in surprise. Jessica gasped as well. I was taking a terrible gamble but I knew it might be my only chance. Or at least the only chance I had before irreparable damage was done to Jessica.

"Tear off his head."

Grinning ear to ear, the bear man advanced on me. I watched him shift and change as he approached, his arms thickening in his loose sleeves and his fingernails growing. Hair burst from his flesh and his loose clothing began to tighten on him.

Right on time, I felt Percy return and press something metal into my hands. I had been convinced I was about to die, and I think Mr. Man-Bear knew it. I figured my sense of smell was better than his, but I was sure he could smell my fear. The fear was gone though, and he looked at me a little strangely beneath extra furry eyebrows as he leaned over me.

I knew what to do this time, and that made it a lot easier. I arced my hand across, surprising everyone that I was not restrained. The knife in my hand had a broken blade, I realized as I swung it, but I had no time to change my swing. It still tore through his neck, spraying some blood even as he staggered back and reached to block it. I did not know if the wound was deep enough to be fatal, but I did know I had less than a second to act if I wanted to press my advantage.

I jabbed the knife into the rope around my ankles. It cut in three sawing motions, then I was lurching to my feet. Jascon was pulling Jessica back with him defensively, and I saw the witch narrow her eyes at me. The raven flew from her shoulder into the air, giving her the freedom to cast whatever flesh eating magic at me she had. I threw the broken knife at her and ducked in front of the still staggering half man, half bear.

He fell to his knees, one hand to his wound and another reaching out for me. I grabbed the giant paw around his wrist and yanked him forward, sending him sprawling onto the ground. I jammed my heel into the back of his head and his neck, then I started running for where I last saw Jessica. He had taken her behind the barricade.

My broken knife had missed his witch. The guards behind me were starting to rush forward at me and she was recovering from her dodge and reaching up into the sky. No doubt she intended to call down some lightning on me or something, I really had no interest in finding out. I changed course and charged her even as she made a throwing motion with her hands at me.

I dove, expecting to be hammered to the ground again at any moment. Instead I felt a rush of air beneath me, as though something large and painful had passed within inches of me. I saw nothing but a flurry of wind against the ground.

I crashed into her thighs, taking her to the ground easily with my heavier weight. She grunted, the air exploding from her lungs as we landed on the hard packed earth. I felt whatever was keeping me separate from the wolf disappear then as well. It rushed into me, restoring my full senses and making me realize I had been missing them since I woke up.

I rose, blood dripping from my hands. The witch would never move again. Beside me her raven fell to the ground, dead before it struck. I turned to look at the soldiers approaching and saw them slow.

My earlier victim was rising to his feet, spitting and coughing up blood as he did so. My stroke had not been deep enough. I growled and nearly went after him, but a fresh whiff of Jessica's scent reminded me of her. I turned and stalked after her, my eyes searching out Lord Jascon.

"I'll kill her," he yelled, turning and holding a dagger to her throat.

"Not while I'm alive you won't," I growled at him.

I saw Jessica looking at me, fear in her eyes. It struck me like an arrow in the heart, for I saw that she was afraid of what I had turned into just as much as she was afraid of the madman holding a knife to her.

I struggled to keep my anger, to keep my change in place. I refused to look at my daughter, knowing I would break and be unable to continue. "As long as you hold her, I can't come for you," I told him. "And no matter how many of your men you send at me, with your witch dead, you know I'll kill them all."

I heard the hacking cough of his defeated champion after I spoke, a testimony to my words. In a fair fight I did not know if I could beat him, but my hackles were raised and right then nothing would stop me.

"Let her go and we'll leave you alone," I offered. "Otherwise there's no place you can hide that I won't hunt you down."

"Daddy," Jessica whimpered, scared for me and of me.

"You expect me to trust you? I've an army of soldiers at your back," he said.

I walked towards him, knowing that none of his army approached me. He stepped back, closer and closer to the edge of the forest surrounding the clearing. I saw now, as I glanced quickly to the side, that the light came from the bridge to my world. The ground shone with an eerie luminescence. Phantom images of the plants in Jess's beautiful garden were superimposed over the otherwise trampled grasses on the ground.

My nostrils flared. I smelled something, something that had escaped me before. Vos was there, hiding somewhere. I had wondered if he had been caught or not. By the anticipation I could smell, I knew he had not. I looked around again, wondering.

When I turned my attention back to Lord Jascon I saw him open his mouth to speak. Instead of words a surprised gasp came out. A blade burst free from his stomach, barely missing Jessica's arm. It was yanked back through and he fell to his knees. My daughter tried to scramble away quickly, but Vos grabbed her arm and held her still. I saw that he had reclaimed his sword from its hiding spot.

"Well done, Eric," he said to me, eyeing me with a mixture of haughtiness and, I thought, pride.

"Let her go," I growled.

"But we had such a good arrangement before," he said convincingly. At least he seemed convinced by it.

"You don't have an army or a kingdom this time," I reminded him.

"I wouldn't be so sure about that," he said, gesturing with his blade at the men behind me. They watched in fascination, curious to see who would come out ahead. I expected them to show outrage for their fallen leader, but instead they seemed more interested in throwing their lot in with the strongest victor. I was reminded again of the mercenary nature of the average Dark Earther.

"I offer amnesty to any that take up service," he called out. "Even to those who don't deserve-"

I started to lunge forward but, changed or not, there was no way I could have crossed the distance. Jascon, still holding the dagger he had threatened Jess with, buried it in Vos' side, below his ribs but at an upward angle. Vos backhanded him with the hilt of his sword, knocking teeth loose and shattering his nose. On the ground, Jascon spat blood and grinned sadistically.

"You'll die with me," he slurred through swelling lips and tongue.

"I'll see you in Hell," Vos growled, driving his sword into him.

Jessica, free, ran to me. She stopped when she got within a few paces, seeing my misshapen features and extra hair. I cringed and felt like the animal I was forever joined with. I forced the hunter away and found that even looking normal again, she eyed me warily.

Vos turned back, one hand going to the knife still stuck in his side. Blood dripped from it and coated his hand. He looked at those assembled and then to me. He took a few awkward steps, then grimaced and closed the distance between us, forcing himself to walk more normally. I could smell the blood and the pain in him, just like I could smell the terror and confusion in Jessica.

"Bastard killed me," he muttered, speaking in low tones because he had little strength for volume. I nodded, hearing the effect the blood filling his lung had.

He turned to look at Jessica and smiled. I could not believe it, the smile lacked its cruel edge. Instead it seemed unfamiliar on him, even awkward. I swallowed against the confused lump in my throat when he turned to me. He jammed his sword into the ground, then laid his hand on my shoulder. He turned me to face the others behind me, the soldiers that only moments ago had been my enemy. Even the man-bear seemed at a loss for a reaction.

"My son," he called out, pausing to try and recapture breath he might never have again. "The eighth Lord Baxter!"

He sagged and without realizing it, my hand went around him to hold him up. He let himself slide to his knees. He pulled the dagger free, breathing a little easier as the blade and a fair amount of blood poured free of his body. He grimaced and looked up at me.

"This place is not like your world," he whispered. "Keep your back to a wall."

I wanted to grab him and shake him. I wanted to tell him to give it to someone else; I had no want or need for it. He sagged again, sliding so that lay on the ground. I knelt beside him, uncertain of what I should do.

"I never wanted her to come to any harm," he whispered, gasping between words for breath that was increasingly hard to come by. "I'd have killed her if I had to–that's what it means to rule."

He reached up and grabbed the rings in my armored shirt. He coughed, blood running from his mouth and speckling my armor and face. He shuddered, overcoming his retching for a moment. Unable to speak, he mouthed the word, "Hunter."

Spasms overcame him then. His body tried to eject the fluid from his lungs, but it was not to be. He jerked a final time and then lay still at my feet. His body, stiff against me, suddenly relaxed. He was gone.

I looked down at him, my mind lost in a swirling ocean of emotions. He had been my father. I had only known him a short time, and in that time there had been more agony, pain, and hatred than friendship, let alone love. Still, I would have liked to have known more. More about my own family's history, even if it was violent and filled with tyranny.

I looked up, blinking away moisture in my eyes that was the result of frustration and feeling I had missed an opportunity. Jessica was there, looking back at me. She had come close and now stood on the other side of Vos' body. She offered me her hand, and even though I could tell she was scared, she was also compassionate and she still loved me. I smiled and took it, then stood up.

I turned to look at the others arrayed against us. They watched me for a long time, then the changeling with the spirit of a bear dropped to one knee. Almost like a wave at a sporting event, the rest followed suit, taking service to me, service I did not want.

"Dad, the sword," Jessica whispered to me.

My stomach clenched in anxiety, my hand found the hilt and I pulled it from the ground, then raised it up in a silent salute, too confused and torn to find any words to use.

Chapter 14

Vos Baxter and Elrik Jascon had been small Lords, from what I had heard. Vos was proud of his realm, but in the greater scheme of the Dark Earth, he was little more than the Lord of a bandit kingdom. Between the two of them, their lands stretched from towns I knew as Marquette to Baraga. A few hundred square miles, including all of the Huron mountains. Beautiful land, especially in a world untouched by strip mining and deforestation caused by lumber mills. And it was mine, if I wanted it.

I did not. I was a fisherman and a father, and that was all I wanted or needed out of life. The portal back to my world was a few feet away. Jessica and I could slip through it with ease and leave it all behind. The bridge would stay open, however, and even worse, it was in my backyard.

Vos and Jascon had both sent men through to establish a stronghold on my world. I had trouble believing they would be able to hold it, given the weapons of destruction humanity in our world had developed. So far I had not seen much that would be able to counter a machine gun or a cruise missile, but allegedly most of Baxter and Jascon's witches and wizards had already crossed over.

It was only the memory of how I had been manhandled by the witches here that made me wonder if they might really be able to hold their ground after all. It filled me with fear for my home; it was filled with innocent and simple people that wanted only to live their lives and enjoy their families and friends. Ambition, to them, involved working some extra hours to put in a sauna or buy a big screen television. It was totally unlike the rapacious greed I had witnessed present in even the youngest of children here.

My father's sword was around my hip now, the scabbard taken from Vos's hips and looped around my own. The many soldiers milled about, uncertain as to what to do. Some officers tried to keep them in line, but without a ruler giving them direction, they began to talk and wonder what the point was. In a short time, I suspected, their thoughts would turn to pillaging what they could and heading back to their homes. Or worse, given the vacuum of leadership I provided, they might be thinking about trying to carve out their own little kingdom.

A chirp and the soft noise of little feet stampeding alerted me to my personal savior. Percy ran and jumped, clinging to Jessica's dress and climbing up it rapidly. She giggled in spite of herself and helped him up onto her shoulder. He sniffed her hair and licked her cheek affectionately.

"Daddy, can we go home now?" I heard Jess asked softly at my side, petting the little guy.

I looked down at her and smiled. It broke my heart to see her hopeful and to know that I had no good answers for her. I wanted to go home, I wanted it like I wanted nothing else now that I had her back. I nodded, not knowing if it was possible or not. "Let's go honey," I said, and turned her to face the magical portal between worlds.

I looked behind me, at the Dark Earth people, and then I turned away and walked with Jess back through the portal. With her crossing over, we would never have to worry about seeing them again. As before, I saw all colors and none, then I had to blink with the sudden realization that I was staring at something that made sense again. Or did it?

I smelled smoke immediately. The garden was as beautiful and full of life as ever, but beyond it trees had been felled and turned into defensive fortifications. Soldiers moved back and forth, dressed in the livery of Lord Baxter.

Smoke still rose from where my house had been. I could not see it, but I knew beyond any doubt that it had been destroyed. I felt my throat close with sudden emotion at the loss of it. We did not have much, but every memory I had of our life together was in there. Every picture and letter, gone forever.

I walked forward, angry again, and felt Jess trailing behind me. "You!" I barked, pointing at a soldier that was closest to me. "What happened here?"

He looked at me, then looked around, wondering who I was and why he should care. "Who are you?" He asked.

"He is the new Lord Baxter," came the growl of the bear-man from behind me. He had come through after us.

I turned and saw him and a few others that had ventured across as well. "Lord Baxter is slain and so is Lord Jascon!" he bellowed to the others, his voice carrying much as I would expect an elephant's trumpet would. "Take a knee to the new Lord Baxter!"

My head swam; I wanted it all to stop. I didn't want anyone taking a knee to me. I just wanted to be left alone.

"Lord Baxter, Sire–the other one, I mean, he sent us here to establish a fort and hold the bridge," the first soldier I had questioned said from where he now knelt.

"Why didn't it shut?" I asked numbly, turning to stare at the garden and the continuing glow that indicated the portal to the Dark Earth.

"The other witches came through," Jessica said in a soft and sullen voice beside me. "They're holding it open now."

"Other witches," I said, trailing off. It was true, Jascon had told me as much. They were spreading out, opening gates of their own for their own nations.

"The fools," I muttered. Then, I turned and spoke loudly, "You're all fools! You can't hope to overcome the armies of this world! They will crush you and then go to your world and ruin what you have! They will take your land and plunder its resources!"

I stood there, staring at the uncomprehending faces of the soldiers before me. My hands clenched and unclenched, until Jessica slipped her hand in mine.

"It's okay," she said with a soft smile. "We can't stay here now, can we?"

I shook my head. "No Jess, it's not okay. It's as far from okay as anything could ever be!"

"Daddy, someone very smart once told me that fair is a concept invented by lazy people that want the same privileges hard working people have, without wanting to do the work."

I looked down at her and in spite of the madness that gripped me, I found myself smiling. I bent down and picked her up, hugging her tightly. I realized she had grown taller in the last couple of years, but I had not been paying enough attention. I squeezed her again then lowered her to the ground. It was a shorter distance than I remembered.

"I don't know what we're going to do, not yet," I told her. "Not while this thing is open."

"Yeah, I know," she agreed. "And even if we could shut the door it's not the same."

"Come on dad, let's go." She said, grabbing my hand again and gently tugging on it. She was pulling me towards the garden.

I turned and looked at the assembled soldiers. I shook my head, then said, "Nobody from this world, Mundania, crosses over. Stand in their way and stop them, do whatever you have to, but nobody gets hurt."

I let that sink in for a moment then said, "I find out anybody is hurt or killed, and you'll wish you had both Vos and Jascon to deal with instead of me."

They saluted, accepting my orders even though they made no sense to them. I could see many questioning looks and I knew that I might have sewn seeds of discontent. Not caring, I turned and walked with Jessica back across the bridge to the Dark Earth.

"My Lord Jascon!"

I looked up, searching for the source of the cry even as my eyes struggled to adjust to the familiar but different scenery. Soldiers parted, some chuckling and others trying to correct the messenger who emerged into the clearing. He saw Vos on the ground first and a smile started to spread across his face, then he saw his liege, Lord Jascon, laying dead behind him. His eyes widened and he looked around, at a loss for what to do.

He turned to Jascon's bodyguard. "Five hundred men from Gharos are here!"

The large man that had tried to kill me grunted and pointed to me. "Tell Lord Baxter, or run."

"Lord Baxter?" He said, looking at me. His eyes fell to the sword at my side, apparently it was well known among these parts. "My Lord," he said, taking a knee after a quick moment where I saw calculating thoughts rush through his mind.

"Who are you?" I asked him.

"Tinse, My Lord," he said quickly, "I was Lord Jascon's adjutant."

I nodded. "What is Gharos?"

"The Kingdom of Gharos is a week's ride to the South, on the SouthWestern edge of Westlake," he informed me.

I connected the fuzzy dots in my head. I remembered hearing the different names of the great lakes here. Northlake was Lake Superior, Westlake was Lake Michigan, and Eastlake was Lake Huron. The Kingdom of Gharos was a large portion of Wisconsin. I remembered Vos mentioning something about it, now that I was thinking about it, and the capital of Gharos was located near the same place I was accustomed to calling Chicago.

"Why are they here?" I asked. I had my suspicions.

Tinse shrugged, though he did so in a deferential way. "I had hoped you might know, My Lord. Perhaps only your predecessor can tell us."

I chewed my lip thoughtfully. There were others he had spoken with. His seneschal, other aides, court staff. People I may have seen in passing but had paid no attention to. I felt like growling, and understood the reason why people cursed. I turned to look at Jessica and found her staring longingly at the gate.

"Go, Jess," I told her, changing my mind. "Go home Princess, I'll make sure nobody comes through."

She turned to look at me, an angry teenage glare in her eyes. "Dad, that's dumb." Ah, the eloquence of youth. "Seriously, you know that won't work! There's going to be other doors opened," she told me. I knew what she was saying, but the certainty in her tone showed me she knew more about it than I did.

"Besides, I'm not leaving you here alone. These people are mean," she added. "Plus I'm not old enough to live by myself."

"You could live with the Tenyke's," I suggested. It was an empty suggestion and I knew it. I hated the thought of being separated from her and I was secretly happy that she was telling me off about it. I was supposed to be older and wiser, but there were times when she and I had to work more as a team than as father and daughter.

She gave me another look that said it all.

"My apologies, My Lord," Tinse said, interrupting with a quiet but urgent tone. "I understand the rumors to be true then, you are, or were, Mundlings?" I scowled at the term but nodded.

"Very well," he said. "That explains it. I would caution you, Sire, not to show weakness in front of others, certainly none other than a trusted few. The men, your vassals, they might think you soft or weak and be rebellious."

I turned on him, suddenly feeling angry again. The hunter was there, urging me on. "I am from another world. A kinder and gentler world, by far. I caution you to never make the mistake of thinking it is a weakness."

He nodded, bowing and taking a step back. I wanted to follow him, berating him further, but I stopped. The eyes of dozens of men were on me, waiting and watching. I swallowed and looked back to my daughter. She nodded encouragingly.

"Not very many girls get to be a real princess when they grow up," she said.

It reminded me of her childhood. I was clueless as the father of a young girl. She loved princesses and fairy tales, so I did my best to keep her buried in them to make her happy. I had thought she might have grown out of it but apparently some childhood dreams never die. Where was my dream of being a mighty lumberjack like Paul Bunyon?

"There's going to be a lot of changes around here," I said, turning to face my witnesses again. I looked back and forth and then walked over to a supply wagon. I climbed up on it so I could see more people and be seen by more of them.

I stood there and opened my mouth, then realized I had no idea what I was supposed to say. I was not a politician. I avoided crowds and the limelight, in fact. I was the captain of a small fishing boat. My crew was two to three people. Now I was staring at maybe a hundred expectant faces. People who seemed to possess very little gratitude, appreciation, decency, or compassion.

"Nobody crosses over," I said finally, speaking loudly enough my voice would carry. "Guards will be posted and without my personal permission, nobody goes through it. Anybody tries, they answer to me."

I was ready to get down, feeling like I had made a fool of myself. I stopped and thought I should say something positive, something uplifting. Something to raise the spirits. Of course I had no such thoughts handy, other than to reassure them that as soon as possible I planned on getting as far away from them as I could.

"Things are going to change around here," I said. "It's a better way of life for all of us, but it's going to take some getting used to and not many of you will like it at first."

I wanted to tell them about democracy and human rights and everything else. The problem was, when it came down to it, I did not know very much about them. I voted when it was convenient and knew about my own basic rights, back on my Earth, at least. Trying to give a civics lesson right then and there seemed like a bad idea. Especially considering their teacher had squeaked through his high school class almost twenty years ago with a C- in the subject. I hopped down and went back to Jessica and Tinse. Bear-man stood nearby, having come back through the gate with us. He looked as large and unmovable as ever.

"You got a name?" I asked him, coming to stop beside him.

"Bulcik," he said, his voice as deep and threatening as I had predicted.

"Bulcik?" I asked rhetorically. He nodded. "All right, why not," I muttered. "Bulcik, you going to be loyal to me or do I need to cut deeper next time?"

His hand went to his throat self-consciously, but he smiled in spite of it. "You bested me," he said, as though that explained everything. Seeing my lack of confidence in his words, he added, "I am bear, our strength is matched only by loyalty to those who we serve."

I nodded. "All right, that's good to know. I hope the day comes soon that I can believe you."

He nodded, slightly offended but moving on in spite of it. "Stay close," I told him. "You're big enough to scare me."

He grinned at my admission, forgetting my slight to him. He followed me, assuming that I had chosen for him to be my personal guard. I had no better job at the moment for him to do. Then again, what I really wanted was for all of them to just leave us alone. "You," I said, pointing at Tinse. "Go through that door, gate, bridge, whatever it is. Round up everybody and tell them to get back here.

"Let's get back to the castle," I said, noticing that Jess was shivering in the cold night air. It was Spring in Northern Michigan, we were lucky it wasn't snowing.

"I'll have a wagon readied for you, My Lord," a guard said, jumping to the chance to make a name for himself.

"Horses, I think, that wagon ride took too long," I said. "Two of them, one for me and one for Jess."

"Can you ride a horse in that getup?" I asked my daughter, turning to her.

She smiled, a genuine smile. "Try and stop me," she said, grabbing the skirts of her robe and swirling them playfully.

Percy made his squirrel noises and even though I knew everything had changed, I also knew that nothing had changed. Nothing that was really important, anyhow.

####

About the Author

Jason Halstead works by day as an IT Professional, developer, and database administrator. From time to time he puts on a few other hats as well.

In his spare time Jason enjoys spending time with his wife and two children, writing, and lifting weights. He enjoys reading and responding to fan mail as well, so if you liked any of his other books, don't be shy!
jasonhals@gmail.com

Other books by Jason Halstead:

Voidhawk
Voidhawk: The Elder Race (coming soon)
Wanted
Ice Princess (coming soon)